BIGFOOT
Stalks the Coast of Maine
and other twisted downeast tales

Other books by Thomas A. Easton:

Fiction:

Sparrowhawk
Greenhouse
Woodsman
Seeds of Destiny
The Tower of the Gods
Unto the Last Generation
Stones of Memory
Silicon Karma
The Electric Gene Machine

Nonfiction:

How to Write a Readable Business Report
Working for Life: Careers in Biology
Careers in Science
Think Thunder! And Unleash Your Creativity
Taking Sides: Clashing Views on Controversial Issues in Science, Technology and Society

Anthology:

Gedanken Fictions

With B. J. Carroll and R. W. Conant (eds.):

Private Means — Public Ends: Private Business in Social Service Delivery

With R. W. Conant:

Cutting Loose: Making the Transition from Employee to Entrepreneur
Using Consultants: A Consumer's Guide for Managers

With Carl E. Rischer:

Bioscope
Focus on Human Biology

BIGFOOT
Stalks the Coast of Maine
and other twisted downeast tales

Thomas A. Easton

WILDSIDE PRESS
Berkeley Heights, New Jersey

First Wildside Press edition: November 2000

BIGFOOT

Stalks the coast of Maine

and other twisted downeast tales

A publication of

Wildside Press

P.O. Box 45
Gillette, NJ 07933-0045
www.wildsidepress.com

FIRST EDITION

Table of Contents

Introduction

I have always been fond of tall tales. That is what first drew me to that genre of popular literature known as science fiction. That, and the ease with which science fiction stretches the bounds of reality. Science fiction (and its cousin fantasy) is fiction for the unfettered mind. It permits the imagination to roam far beyond our daily round, to consider alien beings, distant worlds, strange suns, and unlikely juxtapositions of fact and fancy.

When I returned to Maine in 1977, after a decade in Chicago, I was reminded of how down-to-Earth a land my native state truly was and of how its people can juxtapose fact and fancy much in the way I love. Many Mainers live close to the land, as they always have. They remain unblessed by the feverish prosperity of the Big City and its suburbs, and they are so practical that they could, for instance, take the oil crisis of the early seventies pretty much in stride. They had woodstoves already, though they might be rusting quietly in the barn, and when oil and electric heat became too dear, they remembered how to use the things.

Yet Maine is also a land that can claim Paul Bunyan for its own. Its people love to give an exposed leg a good, hard yank. They applaud good stretchers of the truth, and they even let professional liars (such as Tim Sample and the late Marshall Dodge) make a decent living from their performances.

Maine thus seemed a very fitting place for a science fiction writer to live. Others have agreed — there are Barry Longyear in New Sharon, Stephen King in Bangor, Steve Miller and Sharon Lee in Winslow, Rick Hautala in Westbrook, and others, while Charles Waugh, once one of the field's premier anthologists, lives in Winthrop.

And it wasn't long before I was telling tales about Maine people, especially about the mayor of a certain unnamed coastal town. This mayor bears the name of a late neighbor of mine, an elderly farmer and storekeeper, who was positively delighted to star in tall tales of his own. Practicality personified, he takes the strangest things — from aliens disguised as talking trout to evil wizards, from vampire trees to Bigfoot — in stride. And his adventures have been well received by readers in Maine and elsewhere.

I have used the same juxtaposition of practicality and fancy in other stories than those of *The Alien in the Cider Barrel*, and three of these tales round out this book. “The Bunghole Caper” provides the book’s title. “A Love Story” confronts a newly divorced English professor with a hard-hearted dryad. “Movers and Shakers,” alone of all the tales in this book, is not set specifically in Maine, but it remains very much in the Maine tradition of tall tales.

Mood Wendigo

When did this story begin? It's hard for anyone here in town to say. It looped back on itself and tied its bit of time in a knot. No one is really sure just what happened, though we do know we lost a good boy.

Did it start when Lydia Seltzer told her high school biology class about the wendigo? She was talking about the world's mystery beasts, the Abominable Snowman, the Sasquatch, the Loch Ness Monster and its cousins in other lakes around the world. She told them about all the expeditions, the lack of results, the questions — are the searchers simply crackpots? Or do elusive things still exist in the hidden corners of the world? And then she mentioned the wendigo, a thing that had never been more than a story, a superstition, something no one had ever believed in enough to check it out. Its name was Indian, and it was known across the Northeast, from Maine to Ontario. It screamed in the night, and anyone who sought the screamer disappeared without a trace. If they ever returned, they were mad, too blown of mind even to say what had happened to them. There were no descriptions of the wendigo.

Or did it start the day our town acquired a second Lydia? Mad she was, and raving, but she was the same Lydia we had all known for a decade. The same wide mouth, the nose a little larger than she liked, the black hair worn short and curled over her collar Neither was any beauty, but neither were they ugly, and it seemed surprising that she had never married. Or perhaps it was no surprise after all. She was tough-minded as only a woman can be, and she showed it at an unusually young age. Most women wait till their forties and later to show their steel. But not Lydia. She brooked no nonsense, in class or out, and for as long as we had known her she had been given to severely tailored pant suits, wool for work, denim for evenings and weekends.

When did it start? Who can say? The best I can do is tell you where I came into it. That was some time after the wendigo class. I was at home, sitting at the kitchen table, going over the town budget for the fourth time. Sarah, my wife, was in the living room, watching something inane on TV. We didn't talk much anymore, not about her job at the bank, nor about mine. We had no kids.

When the buzzer sounded, I heard her chair creak as she rose to answer the door. There was a murmur of voices, steps in the hall, and "Harry? Miss Seltzer wants to see you." There was a glare with the words. I ignored it, raised my head from the papers and said, "Duty calls, then. Have a seat, Lydia. Coffee, a drink?"

"Do you have any tea?" As Lydia pulled the other chair out from the table, Sarah disappeared. A moment later, the sound of the TV rose, as if to drown out anything that might give my wife's fantasies the lie. But my attention was for Lydia. She seemed more serious than usual, if possible and there was a folded paper jutting from her bag. I wondered what was on her mind as I filled the kettle. I found out soon enough.

She sat still, watching me as I moved about the room, saying nothing until our tea was before us and I had sat down again. Then she said, "Mayor, I need a leave of absence. A short one."

She stirred her cup, squeezed the bag and dumped it in the ashtray half full of my pipe ashes. "Of course," I said: "But shouldn't you be asking the superintendent about this?" I was puzzled. It wasn't my chore to handle the teachers, thank goodness. I was the town's unpaid mayor, and there were professionals, paid ones, to handle day to day affairs.

"I will," she replied. She looked at me, her brown eyes unblinking. I remember thinking that for all her mannishness she would be worth shielding from all grief. Perhaps it was the eyes. Maybe it was just Sarah. "But you can help," she said "You know people, and . . ."

"But what do you need help with?"

She shrugged and took the paper from her bag. She unfolded it and handed it to me. "Look at this," she said. "It's French-Canadian, a rhyme, collected back in the thirties by the WPA people. I found it in the university library, buried in the folklore files."

The paper was covered with a pencilled scrawl, a copy of a poem that must have been set down by someone who wished to capture the flavor of a speech pattern:

Ze Wendigo,
Zat crazy beast,
'E never eats,
But loves t'go.

In darkest night,
'E runs and screams
And stirs ze dreams
Of second sight.

But when you go
To join ze run,
'E stays unknown,
Ze Wendigo

I packed and lit my pipe, studying the rhyme, before I spoke "Interesting," I said. I sent a cloud of smoke toward the ceiling. "But what does it have to do with a leave of absence?"

Her fingers tensed around her tea cup. She had come to me, but she seemed unwilling to reveal her problem. Could it be so rare or odd or shameful? Suppose it was, I told myself, and then I guessed the answer.

"You want to go wendigo hunting." I laughed.

Her lips tightened, and I was immediately sorry for the laughter. That was just the reaction she had feared. Of course. No one wants to be thought a nut, a crackpot, even if their ideas are a bit off the beaten track. "But go on," I said, trying to save the situation. "Maybe I can help. At least, I'm game to try."

She relaxed as if that was all she had wanted. I caught a faint whiff of perfume or cologne. And she began to talk. She told me of the wendigo class, of her own interest in the strange, of her sense of fairness that led her to the library, of her conviction that all the legends must reflect some grain of truth, of her wish to seek that truth. She had come to me for suggestions on where to seek, a guess at the chances of success, perhaps even a partner in the strange quest.

Why me? Well, I do have a reputation for imagination. Last year's ad program for my oil business certainly stirred folks up enough. And then there were the gimmicks I had come up with to get more tourists into the area. And then, too, there had been a few incidents now and again to connect me with the strange. Really, I should have been more surprised if Lydia had not come to me.

But what could I do? I wouldn't know a wendigo if I saw one. Or heard one, rather. She was silent while I relit my pipe and thought. She didn't fidget much, only turning her empty cup back and forth between her hands. Finally, I said, "There's at least one fellow in this town who could help. If you'll come to the town hall tomorrow after school, I'll ask him to meet us there."

She nodded and sighed. Her breath whistled as if she had been holding it. So I would help, after all. Her voice was softer when she spoke. "Do you really think we can. . . ?"

"How can we know?" I grimaced, sympathetically, I hoped. "We've no idea what it looks like or where to look. But we can try."

The fellow I wanted to talk to was Howie Wyman. Grizzled, always overalled and booted, he had been doing odd jobs as long as anyone cared to recall. He knew all the stories, too, though he didn't talk much. He seemed to prefer the woods and streams to human company, even his wife, but he was in town at the time, painting a house over on Water Street. I sent a secretary to ask him to come by a little after three.

I was still alone when he showed up, a motley collection of paint spatters, whiskers, and faded cloth completely alien to any civilized conception of a government office. My secretary showed him in, though, as if he were clad in a three-piece suit and fresh from the barber, which tells you something about our town. It's informal. Partly because it's small and partly because its people waste little energy on nonessential appearances. They dress up mostly for church and they try to keep their drinking private.

I said, “Thank you, Bonny,” and waved Howie to a seat. He took it, looked for my wastebasket, and got rid of his wad of chewing tobacco. “You wanted me, Mayor.”

“Ayuh.” I said. “Lydia Seltzer dragged me in on a project of hers. I thought you might be able to tell us something helpful.”

“Like what?” He looked doubtful. He knew Lydia was the science teacher, and he knew nothing about science. I doubted he’d ever gotten past the sixth grade. I was starting to tell him about the problem when Lydia walked in, Bonny holding the door until I waved at her. Her wool was pink today. and her face was flushed with eagerness. The combination wasn’t attractive, but I didn’t imagine it was anything but temporary. I hoped she wouldn’t be disappointed.

I introduced Howie to Lydia. “This is the fellow I was talking about. I was just going to tell him the problem.”

She took the other chair. “Shall I go on, then?” When I nodded, she produced that paper again and then handed it to Howie. While he read, she said what she wanted, flatly and directly. The nervousness I had seen last night was gone.

When she finished, Howie set the paper on the corner of my desk and said simply, “Pork Hill.” I raised my eyebrows, and he went on. “My dad was up there once. Ayuh, huntin’ deer in the dark of the moon. He heard that scream. Didn’t see nothin’, though.”

“Where’s Pork Hill?”

“North by west, ‘bout ten miles.”

And that was all he had for us.

We now had a place to look, and the next dark of the moon was just two weeks away, in case that mattered. Lydia could hardly wait. She insisted on borrowing a tent, sleeping bags, a Coleman stove, all the gear anyone could want for a night camping on a lonely hilltop. She got most of it from two members of the school board. She got their sons, too. Keith Hutchison and Ronny Jackson were two of her best students, and she thought they deserved a field trip, a little hands-on research. They thought so too, especially since it meant a Friday away from school. I didn’t argue, since I was sure we could meet no danger from a superstition.

I wish I had been right. Keith was a lanky boy, tall, a forward on the school basketball team. Ronny was shorter, sturdier, a soccer player. Both had family, friends, girl friends, good prospects. Keith, in fact, already had a scholarship for college. They had a lot to lose, but they were eager. Danger was just a myth, and they wouldn’t miss this trip for worlds.

They didn’t, of course. I didn’t believe in any danger myself, so I didn’t try to talk them out of it, and Lydia made it sound like a lark. All the way up there, the four of us and the gear crowded into my old station wagon, she waved her camera and ran on about the splash a picture of a real, live wendigo would make.

We loaded the car on Thursday night and left town shortly after noon on Friday. When we met in the town hall lot, I was surprised to see Lydia in dungarees and a red-checked wool shirt. It was so unlike her that, even though the rest of us were dressed similarly, she seemed to stand out. But the clothes were suitable for the trip, and I soon stopped noticing them.

It took us half an hour to reach the foot of Pork Hill, and another two hours to hump the gear to the top. The hill wasn't big, no more than eight hundred feet high, but it was steep and wooded and there was no path. The going was slow until we reached the top, where the trees disappeared. Pork Hill was one of those rocky knobs scattered over the state of Maine, its top scraped clean by glaciers and still inhabited only by lichen, moss, blueberry bushes, and a few stunted birches.

We pitched the tent in a mossy hollow between boulders, and the boys went back down the hill to gather firewood. There were plenty of fallen branches there, and though we had the stove, a fire was a comforting thing to have at night. Even small mountains can get chilly after dark.

By suppertime, the woodpile was large enough to last a week. We had all taken time to explore the hilltop, too, following Lydia as she sought some clue to what a wendigo might be, some trace of something strange. We found nothing but glacial scours and animal droppings and a few weathered shotgun shells, though Lydia was hardly discouraged. As she said when the boys were finally kindling their fire, "It is a traveler, they say. Maybe it never stops here."

I said something which I now wish I hadn't. Though it probably didn't change a thing. "Then you'll have to move quickly to get a picture of it. It won't be waiting for you."

"I suppose I will," she said, fingering the camera on its strap around her neck. She bent, then, to the totebag she had brought and extracted a flash, one of those electronic ones that don't need bulbs. "I'd better be ready."

We ate — hamburgers and potato salad and coffee and bakery pie — and sat around the fire staring, satisfied for the moment by the mystery of its flames. Only Lydia turned her head now and again to the darkness, straining to see what she waited for. But there was nothing but the odor of earth and growing things, the sight of stars like raindrops on a windshield. The air turned chill enough for sweaters, and we listened to the chirps and buzzes of insects, the lazy notes of sleepy birds, the small croaks of tree frogs, and the rare crackling of brush as some animal — deer, coon, rabbit, coyote, even a wild house cat — passed within hearing.

We talked, of what it meant to be a mayor or a teacher or a student, of sports and fishing and hunting, of politics and taxes. We told no ghost stories, though. I suppose that must have been because our mission was too much like such a tale. It would have been tempting fate to describe horrors and frights, and fate never needed tempting.

Eventually, we talked ourselves out and let the fire die. We were readying ourselves for the sleeping bags, washing up, brushing teeth, when it happened. We heard a moan at first, low as if far distant, swelling loud and clear and close. At its peak it sounded like a baby must when it is being dipped in boiling oil.

It was a little after midnight and as black as the inside of a closet. We had been using the light of an electric lantern as well as the glow of the coals. We had been contained in a small and cozy room, but that sound broke down the walls. I shuddered, and Lydia ran, the soap and water spilled on the moss, her camera ready in her hand, Keith hot on her heels. Ronny would have gone too, but I held him still with a hand on his shoulder. "Let go!" he cried. "I want to see it too!"

"Remember the stories," I said as softly as I could over the dying scream. "Someone should mind the camp." He subsided as I'd hoped he would. When the scream was gone and the night was again silent, I added, "Now. Now we can look for them."

We took our flashlights and tried to follow the marks Lydia and Keith had crushed into the moss as they ran. But the tracks soon disappeared in the tangled skein of prints we had made earlier that afternoon. We called and shouted. We covered every inch of that hilltop, again and again, shining our lights down cracks in the rock and under bushes, checking the bottom of every drop we came across, large or small. We searched until our batteries were exhausted, and then we huddled around a rebuilt fire, worrying, starting at every crackle of brush.

With the dawn, we searched and called again, but we had no better luck. Lydia and Keith had vanished without a trace, just as in the legends. I was closer than ever before to believing in the wendigo, and thus in ghosts, banshees, and all the rest of what I had once dismissed as so much claptrap.

Our second search soon ended in futility. We made a hasty breakfast, doused the fire, and broke camp. Then we lugged the gear back to the car. It took longer, since there were fewer of us now. I had plenty of time to berate myself, to think I should never have helped Lydia with her obsession, never have let the boys come along, never have come myself. But who could have expected a myth to be real? Who could have guessed it would cost us half our party? And what was the wendigo? What was it that made a sound that swelled and faded like a freight train's whistle, that screamed like a soul in torment? Like a god on a cosmic treadmill? If only I had known, I might have left the boys in town, but I would still have come with Lydia, hoping to protect her, shield her. I felt as I might for the child I didn't have, and I mourned.

Ronny was less thoughtful. He shivered when he thought of the night, and once he dropped his load with a clatter of pans. He had lost a teacher and a friend. He might have been lost himself. The horror of that scream had almost touched him, and he could barely control his thoughts. He stayed close to me, keeping a wary eye on the woods around us, talking endlessly, trying to imagine what had happened to the others. He failed to disrupt my thoughts only because I was as obsessed myself. There was no conversation. He talked on, while I muttered responsive noises, and we both scurried around our separate skulls, like rats seeking the way out of a trap.

By mid-morning, we were back in town. I stopped the car in front of the town hall. The police station was across the street. We would have to go there first, of course. Missing persons, runaways, lost in the woods, carried off by a mythical beast, had to be reported, search parties organized, motions gone through even if they could do no good. Ronny was still talking, muttering, his skin a cold and clammy white, his eyes glazed. I helped him out of the car and steered him across the road. I remember being glad he hadn't collapsed while we had work to do. It would have been a shame to leave all that gear on top of Pork Hill.

Our town's Chief of Police was a heavy-bellied man whose moon face wore a thin moustache. He was young, about thirty, and as competent as we needed. Most of his energies were spent on rounding up drunks and vandals, occasional burglars, and the odd con man. He could do the work because the town was small and the crime rate low, but he could never hope to improve his lot. He would grow old in the job, the gut would sag, the cheeks jowl and the eyes go piggish. The tattoos on his forearms would fade, and somewhere along the line we would have to get rid of him. I wouldn't miss him; no one would. His sense of social class was far too keen.

When we entered his office, he rose and said, "G'morning, Mayor! I thought you were going wendigo hunting yesterday?"

"We did," I said shortly.

"Ah!" He grinned jovially, as if we shared some secret. "Stealing a march on your great white huntress, hey?"

"Whatever do you mean?" I asked. I was irritated by his tone, impatient with what had to be nothing but nonsense. But his next words set me back. "Lydia Seltzer. She didn't go with you."

It didn't sound like a question, but what else could it be? "Of course she did. That's why I'm here now. She disappeared last night. She and Keith Hutchison."

The Chief plopped his bulk back into his swivel chair. He looked startled. "But . . ." Then he paused, looking at Ronny as if for the first time. "What's the matter with him?"

"Shock and exhaustion," I said. "We were up all night, searching for them. Maybe one of your men would get him over to the hospital and tell his parents where he is."

"Of course, Mayor." He pushed a button on his desk intercom. Then he said, "Maybe you'll tell me what happened when . . ." A patrolman entered, was given his instructions, and left with Ronny. The Chief turned back to me. "Now," he said.

I gave him the story. He nodded when I was done. "The shock I can understand," he said. "But why didn't you get here hours ago?"

"I didn't think it wise to go stumbling through the woods in the dark. Besides, I hoped we might find something in the morning."

"Not that it really makes a difference. A search party wouldn't do any good."

"Why not? They could still be there someplace! Maybe they fell in a hole we didn't see, or got lost in the woods."

"No." He shook his head and rose again. "C'mon. I'll show you."

He led me back to the small cell block. When we entered the narrow corridor, lined with steel bars, I could hear a noise, a jabbering sound, wordless, random. Or almost random. As he steered me toward the noise, I began to pick out shreds that might hold meaning: "fetal train," "stars and stars," "hopper freight," "take yon train," and more, though those were clearest. I wondered what madman he was holding here. And then we faced the last cell in the row. Through the bars, I made out a form strapped onto the narrow bunk, head tossing, face bruised and scratched, denim and wool clothes torn and soiled. It was Lydia.

The Chief spoke. "We picked her up like that yesterday afternoon. She walked into town, went straight to the school, and tried to get into her classroom, raving all the time, just like this. The substitute called the principal, and he called us. I'm waiting for the judge to sign the papers now, and then one of the men'll drive her to Augusta."

AMHI. The Augusta Mental Health Institute. Where they would try to bring her back, perhaps with drugs and electric shocks. But what else could anyone do? I turned away.

Back in the Chief's office, I remembered Lydia's camera. Did he have it? He did, along with everything that had been in her pockets. "Then perhaps," I said, "it might be a good idea to have the film developed. She could have got her pictures after all, and they could help the doctors understand what's wrong with her now."

"Of course," he said, and I left. I wanted sleep, but I should return the gear Lydia had borrowed first and tell Keith's family what had happened. Then, maybe, I could begin to puzzle over how Lydia had disappeared last night and reappeared yesterday. Time travel was impossible, wasn't it?

The Hutchisons and Jacksons were enraged. With me, with Lydia, with the town, with the school. One boy lost, another ill, but the lost one most on their minds. Jack Hutchison swore he would run against me come the next election, sue me for every penny I had, have Lydia fired if she ever regained her wits. But the prospect of no longer being mayor didn't bother me — after all, it didn't pay — and the trip had officially been a school field trip, and the school had insurance to cover lawsuits.

And then that fuss died down. The pictures came out. Lydia had her wendigo, twice. One shot showed a line of shiny boxes stretching down a gleaming tunnel. The other showed Keith walking away from the camera, hand in hand with a figure that wasn't human, through a vast cavern of a room. The shiny boxes covered the floor of that room, and they were surrounded by machines that bore vague resemblances to freight dollies and forklift trucks.

I could guess what the wendigo really was. An interstellar freight train, its tracks looping close to Earth at certain times and places, a freight that could be hopped by anyone who got too close to its passing field. "Fetal?" Maybe "ftl," faster than light. By "take yon" had she meant "tachyon?" I read enough to know what that was, how it might fit, and Keith was alive and well, Earth's envoy to other worlds. Lydia, on the other hand, had been sent back on the next train, going faster than light, backward in time just enough to get her home a day before she left.

By the time Lydia stopped raving and returned to her job, Pork Hill could no longer be visited, either by deer poachers or by would-be interstellar hobos. The army had taken it over, and it was now ringed by wire fence and armed guards while the experts tried to find a way to flag some passing train down.

I don't know if they'll succeed. Lydia can't tell us anything, since she now seems to have no memory of her journey, and if it weren't for that last picture of Keith I'd be tempted to compare us to the moose. For years, the rutting bulls would answer train whistles by charging down the tracks into the engine. To the bull moose, it seems, the whistles sounded like the cry of a cow in heat, and they never learned the difference. The slaughter only stopped when the companies changed the note of the whistles.

But we can't be the equivalent of animals running head-on against an oblivious technology. After all, who among us would walk out of a railway station hand in hand — or hoof in hand — with a moose?

The Tree

It was a warm May Friday, with the air full of apple blossoms and bay mud, and Joelle Dobson did not have her mind on what she was doing.

She had come into my office a couple of weeks ago to say she was curious about her family's house. The superstructure, she said, was fairly new but the foundation of roughly trimmed granite boulders was not. And too, she'd been bothered by folks' reactions when they learned where she lived. An old woman she'd met in church had shaken her head sadly and said, "Pity. You look like such nice people, too." No one would say anything more.

I hadn't been able to give her much help. But the town clerk had loaned her a desk and showed her how to use the town records. Since then, she had been as diligent as any scholar, spending most afternoons with dusty tomes, ferreting out previous owners, changes in property descriptions, and so on.

But today, every time I passed the large room in which the clerks worked, she was just sitting there, staring out the window. It nagged at me, and eventually I laid down my pen, pushed my paperwork aside, and left my office. I passed Bonny's desk, where she sat to guard my door, and went down the stairs. I touched Joelle's shoulder. "Something wrong?" I asked.

She shook her head, but she wasn't saying no. "Chrissy's in the hospital."

I squeezed the shoulder. "Then why don't I pay her a visit? Want to come?"

"Later on. Sam's there now."

I didn't take the car. It was only a mile to where Chrissy was housed, I told myself, and the walk would give me time to think, to feel the town whose Mayor I was, to bitch to myself about the cash flow problem that goes with selling fuel oil. Not that I wasn't enjoying the warmth. I was. But I wasn't paid for being Mayor. I had to make my living somehow.

Chrissy was on the second floor, adrift in odors of alcohol and clean linen and soap, with a room of her own. The door was ajar. I knocked, heard her soft "Come in," and entered. Her father, in the armchair by the window, said, "Hello, Harry."

"Hi, Sam," I said. I didn't look at him. The room was dim, the curtains half drawn, and the single lamp over the bed spotlighted the patient. Chrissy, blonde and six years old, was leaning against a pillow. The head of the bed was raised. She wore a flowered nightgown and held a coloring book on her lap. And she was pale, very pale. “Hi, Chrissy.”

The hospital hadn’t stolen her impish grin. “Harry!” I crossed the room and shook her hand. Then I propped my backside against her bed and let her tell me about how being sick got you new toys and books and even friends. “There’s a man just down the hall,” she told me. “He’s old, like Grampa. He’s sick too.”

I said something about that’s what hospitals were for, to make sick people well. She shook her head vigorously, her hair flying. “He’s going to die,” she said. “But not like the cat.”

“What cat?”

“The one in the yard, by Mr. Oak Tree.” Her face was solemn. “Its neck was twisted.” She twisted her hands together to show me what she meant. I gave her a shudder, and she grinned at me. Like most kids, she loved to have grown-ups appreciate her performances.

Then Sam spoke. “Somebody must have thrown it from a car,” he said. I looked at him. His face too was solemn, a trace of upset still lingering from whenever they had found the cat. “Happened last week,” he added.

I nodded and rolled my eyes toward the door to the hall. Would he tell me more before I left? He nodded back, and I returned my attention to Chrissy. We chatted for a few minutes more, I told her to get well real soon, and then we said good-bye.

Sam walked me out of the room and down the hall to the stairs. At the door, he turned to face me. “That cat isn’t the only strange thing that’s happened lately,” he said. I rummaged in a pocket for my pipe and tobacco. I couldn’t light up in the hospital, but once I was outdoors. . . .

Sam Dobson was the manager of our local bank. He wasn’t particularly handsome. His eyebrows were too thick and turned under as they neared his nose. The nose itself had a dogleg from college football. His teeth were crooked, and the right side of his lower lip was thickened by a small knot of scar tissue. At five-eleven, he was a little taller than me, and he carried more weight than he should. “Chrissy’s illness?” I asked.

He raised one hand to brush at his sandy hair. “That’s part of it, I suppose,” he said. “She’s got a rash on her front. Anemic, too. And the doctors can’t figure why.”

I snorted. “That’s nothing new.”

He shrugged. “They do say it’s nothing serious. She’s getting better already. But she’s still having the nightmares.”

I raised my eyebrows.

“Started after we found the cat. She woke up screaming it wanted her, too.” He hesitated. “That’s when she started losing her appetite, getting listless. And then she got the rash.”

I thought that over for a minute. It didn’t seem to make much sense. “Anything else?”

He shrugged again. “Noises in the dark. Tappings on the windows. Wind, you know? And there's dirt on the window sills, as if Chrissy's been climbing on them. And she's a pretty good girl. We've told her not to climb, but the dirt's still there. She doesn't even try to clean it up."

This was curious. "Footprints?" I asked.

He shook his head. I studied his face. I could see frustration in it, uncertainty. He wasn't used to mysteries. Money was more like it, numbers on paper and computer disks, rigidly controlled by the laws of arithmetic. I said something I hoped would calm him down, and then I left.

I didn't feel much like eating that night. I did feel like company, though, and there was only one place in town to find that after about eight. I headed to Rollie's Cafe, the tavern on lower Main Street.

Rollie's was a long, dim room behind dirty plate glass. It stank of stale smoke and grease and beer. It held a bar to one side, stools, and a number of tables just big enough for elbows and glasses. Most of the tables were empty when I walked in, but one held two old friends, Howie Wyman and Andy Hanks. I headed for them.

"Evenin', Mayor," said Andy. Tall and skinny, with a road-map face, he ran the local lumberyard.

"Evenin', yourself." Howie pushed a third chair out with a foot. I took it. "Where's Emma, Howie?" I hadn't expected to find him there. Dressed in his usual checked shirt, dirty overalls, and leather boots, a felt hat shoved back on his head, he looked like a congenital bachelor. He was married, though, and Emma tried to keep a close rein on him. She wasn't too successful. He worked when he liked, helping at harvest, house-painting, and such. He preferred fishing and hunting.

"Winterport," he said. "Visitin'."

"Ayuh." When I had ordered my hamburger and beer from Rollie, the ex-boxer who ran the place, Howie said, "Where's Sarah?"

"Home." Sarah was my wife.

"Fight?"

"Ayuh." He nodded and I said, "Though I'd rather talk about something else."

The two of them looked at me expectantly. The next move was up to me. I retrieved my pipe from my pocket, stared at it for a moment, and lit it. Then I told them what Sam Dobson had told me.

Andy shifted uneasily in his seat. Howie watched him as he told me, "That house never did have much of a reputation."

Joelle had told me as much, but I didn't know why. The Dobsons had bought the Townsend place two years before. Sam had told me one reason why they liked it was the lone oak tree in the corner of its front lawn. The tree was over a yard thick at the base, its branches arched over lawn and street alike, and it had named the street: Oak Lane. It might have been as old as the town itself.

I said something doubtful. Andy looked away before telling me, "Don't think anyone's ever had the place more'n five-six years."

"So why'd they sell?"

"Didn't, most of 'em," said Howie.

"Died?"

"Ayuh. Or they had a fire and left it to the town for taxes. Ain't nobody's had it longer'n old Tolman Carter."

"I suppose he was the first."

"Ayuh. Used to call it the Carter place."

"When was that?"

"God knows," said Andy. "Ain't been Carters in this town since my Daddy was a boy. Just as well, too."

My food came, I set down my pipe, and the talk turned to other matters. The trout season was still new, and Howie had been doing well. So had I, for that matter. Andy didn't fish, but he had a crew putting up a few houses on spec, and he had that to talk about.

By the time we were done, I was mildly looped on the beer. It would be embarassing, I thought, to pick up a police escort on the way home, but the hell with it. We parted on the sidewalk, and I got into my car.

On the way home, I told myself that now I'd be able to give Joelle Dobson a hand.

When I reached the office Monday morning, Bonny was already there. I had hired her the year before, but only partly for her secretarial skills. She was easy on the eyes, tall and dark-haired, not too slim, comfortably curved. She wore her hair short and combed it to frame intelligent, sympathetic eyes. Her mouth seemed soft and luscious, and her voice was as gentle as a good white wine. Her largish nose detracted not at all.

The phone rang while I was settling at my desk. I heard Bonny get it, the murmur of her voice. I stared at the stack of paperwork waiting for me. I didn't feel much like tackling it. Maybe it would help if I went fishing?

The door swung open and I turned my head to watch Bonny enter the room. She was smiling, a cream skirt swirling around her knees. She said, "Paul Johnson. He'll be dropping around in awhile."

Paul was my lawyer, but he did a little work for the town too. There was no telling what he wanted. He might even want to go fishing, though he was more the hunter, one week a year in deer season. Dressed for that, all brown and plaid except for the orange cap, prematurely grey, he would sometimes say that the thick scar marring his left cheek was a reminder not to run guns anymore.

When he came in, I asked Bonny to bring coffee, and the two of us passed the time of a slow day. We said nothing very interesting until I asked him what he knew about the Dobsons.

"Well," he said. "I do some work for the bank. And Sandra and I do live just down the street from them. Know 'em pretty well, I guess."

"Ah. You hear anything about Chrissy?"

"Ayuh. She's doing a lot better. Home today, I hear. The twins'll be happy for that. They play together."

That afternoon, I stopped downstairs at the town clerk's office. Joelle Dobson was at her borrowed desk, a red-cornered, leather-bound deed register open before her. Its ink was a faded brown, so it was one of the older ones.

For all her French name, Joelle was as red-haired and green-eyed as an Irish colleen. She had the freckles, too, and fine, red lips over small, even teeth. She wore button earrings with denim slacks and shirt, and her hair curled around a face that might have been pushed off center by a gentle fist. She wasn't tall, and her waist was thicker than it might have been, but her face gave her beauty of a sort. It certainly caught the eye.

I pulled up a chair and told her the little I'd learned from Howie and Andy. She grinned at me and pointed at her notes. "I'd just got that far this morning. Old Tolman Carter, first settler, built in 1650. Maybe he even put in that foundation. He lived there fifty years before his granddaughter inherited it. She stayed for twenty. The next one stayed twenty-five, and then the times started getting shorter."

I was intrigued. "Five years, average?"

"It's been that for almost two hundred years."

"And fires and deaths account for it."

"But why?"

"Indian curse?"

"Hah."

"How's Chrissy?"

"Fine, now. I'll pick her up and take her home as soon as I'm done here." She looked relieved.

"Then you'd better move it, eh?"

By the time I made it back to the office, I had had a thought. The town library had a town history or two. There might even be some old diaries. I stopped in Bonny's room. She said, "Coffee?" I nodded, and while she was getting it, I said, "You have enough slack in the day to do a little library work, don't you?" When she nodded as she turned away from the pot atop the bookcase, I told her what Joelle was looking for. "See what you can find?" She agreed. She could. She would. Tomorrow.

For some reason, I couldn't sit still that night. When I could stand it no longer, I went for a drive. I headed out of town, taking the back roads that led past my favorite trout streams. I saw deer in the headlights, rabbits, and once a family of coons bumbling along beside the road. I stopped at Willett Brook. I got out and stared down at the big pool below the bridge. The trout were rising. I picked a moth off a headlight and tossed it in. It was greeted by a splash. There were some big fish there, I told myself. I would have to come back soon with my gear.

The next evening I went for another drive, this time around the town, along the streets and alleys, past fading mansions and trim capes and unpainted wrecks and vacant lots. I was passing Wilson's Grocery, at the foot of Oak Lane, for the third time when I saw Sam Dobson. He was walking from the store toward home, carrying a paper sack. I pulled up beside him, stuck my head out the window, and said, "Hey, Sam. Want a ride?"

He hefted his sack, said, "Milk," and went around the car to get in. When he was seated, I asked, "How's Chrissy?"

"She had nightmares again last night." He sighed heavily in the dark and leaned his head against the rest. "I wish. . . ."

"There's no telling what about?"

He shook his head. "Just something after her. We tried warm milk. Why we ran out."

I stopped in front of his house. There was a hedge along the walk. Over it I could see warm light spilling from the living room windows. He opened his door and said, "Want to come in awhile?"

I shook my head, but I did turn off the engine. "Not tonight, Sam. Though I'll stretch my legs with you for a second." We both got out. We stood side by side on the sidewalk. We stared up at the house.

He pointed at the second story. "That's Chrissy's room. The corner by the tree."

I followed his finger. Her window was open a crack. A streetlight reflected off the glass. A tree branch stretched toward the window. It came so close that its final twigs actually seemed to be reaching through the crack into the room.

He said, "I'll have to prune it this summer. Comes too close to the house. Keeps us up when the wind blows."

"Ayuh. Might get Howie Wyman to do it for you."

"I might at that. I hear he's cheap."

"Does good work, too."

Wednesday morning, Bonny reported that she had found three town histories in the library. One was good; two were full of hearsay and legends and tall tales. All three told the tale of the Townsends. John Townsend had founded the town bank in 1885. His son James took it over in 1915, bought what had been the Carter place in 1920, built a fine house on the old foundation, and lived there until 1924, when an aunt dropped in to find his wife and three sons strangled. James was out of town at the time, with a perfect alibi, but suspicion ruined him and the bank. He sold the house and left town. The new owners held the place less than three years; it burned in 1927, with no survivors.

The oldest of the histories claimed the Carter place was under a curse. There was more, too, but nothing to explain the mystery. And the mystery wasn't anything I wanted to tell the Dobsons about. Maybe later, since Bonny did say she wasn't done yet. "The library has some old diaries," she told me. "Liz thinks one might be Tolman Carter's. She's looking for it." Liz was the librarian.

It was late that afternoon when Sam called me at the office. Could I come over right away? He had something to show me. I said, "Yes," and hung up. I looked at the clock. The bank had been closed for over an hour. So he meant the house.

I didn't waste any time. Bonny's report had bothered me, and I didn't like what seemed to be happening around the Dobsons. I dropped what I was doing, told Bonny where to find me, and headed for the parking lot.

I was at the Dobsons' within ten minutes. I stopped the car beside the curb. There didn't seem to be anything wrong. Past the side of the house, I could see Chrissy in the back yard. The Johnson twins were with her, and they seemed to be having a fine time. Joelle and Sandra Johnson were there, too. Then a movement by the hedge, near the tree, caught my eye. Sam stood up. He waved to me. "Over here."

I got out of the car and joined him. When I got close enough to see over the hedge, I noticed Paul Johnson down on his knees. He looked up at me.

I found a squirrel this afternoon," said Sam. "Strangled, just like that cat."

"That's not all, either," said Paul. He waved a hand toward the roots of the hedge. "I started poking around in here." With one hand he raked a pile of whitish sticks toward me.

I knelt, Sam beside me. I looked closer. The whitish sticks were bones. Paul prodded at a scatter of stony lumps. "Skulls," he said. "Two more cats. A dog. Couple woodchucks. Squirrels. Rats. Birds. God knows what else."

I reached for a fistful of moldy hedge litter. It was impossible not to. What else might be there? I dug out small bones and skulls, and then I uncovered something larger. It looked like the end of a thigh bone, but a small one. I dug some more. I pulled. It came loose. "A big one," said Sam. "Dog?"

"I hope so," I said. I stared at him. A presence loomed over us. I could feel it, feel it yearning. I glanced up at the tree. I stood and backed away. They came with me.

Paul's voice was soft as he said, "I have a chainsaw, Sam."

Sam shook his head. "I don't believe it," he said.

"I don't either, but. . . ."

"But I might move Chrissy to the other end of the house."

"You do that."

He turned to me. "The rash was back this morning. And she was pretty listless."

"Until the twins came over," said Paul.

"Right." Sam grinned. "Can't be too serious, then, can it?"

"Ayuh," I said. "Movin' her won't hurt, though."

"Sure won't."

"Might even help."

I didn't like it. Not a bit. I even called up Howie to tell him so. When I finished, he was silent for a moment. Then he said, "Might be smart to take another look.

Tonight. Be right there."

A quarter of an hour later, Howie's battered pick-up pulled into my drive. I met him as the engine dieseled to a halt, said, "Well?" and waited while he spat his chaw of tobacco onto the lawn. He climbed out and said, "Pretty dry. Got a drink?"

Typical. We went inside. I got out the jug and poured something for each of us. Then I said, "Thought you wanted to have a look?"

"Ayuh," he said. He took a hearty swig of his glass. "Good bourbon, Harry. No rush."

"Why not?"

He shrugged. "Can't rightly say."

All right. I knew Howie. He had a feeling, that was all. But I knew his feelings were to be trusted. He had an affinity for strange events, and an intuitive understanding well beyond my grasp. The closest I could come was a sometimes calm acceptance, and it had taken me years to achieve it.

So we had our drinks. We had another. I told him more of what was going on, and he told me of the banshee of Mill Hollow, probably a feeble-minded flasher a century before his time, but. . . .

In time, we made it into town and to the Dobson's. We paused on the walk long enough to get a good look at the tree. It looked like a tree, nothing more. We knocked. Sam let us in, took us out to the kitchen, and handed us beers. He and Joelle were already equipped. He raised his in my direction. "Got Chrissy into the guest room," he said. "She seemed relieved."

"Then you shouldn't have any trouble tonight," I guessed.

Howie grunted. When I looked at him, he said, "I dunno. Somethin' queer goin' on."

Sam nodded as if he hadn't smelled Howie's — and my — breath when we came in. Joelle's eyes widened. His comment hadn't helped her. She said, "What do you mean?"

Howie waved his beer in the air. "Your tree. 'Tain't what it seems. Can't be."

We chewed on that, silently, while Joelle turned pale and paler and Sam tightened his mouth grimly. We drank our beers.

I tried to break the silence by saying, "You should have seen the bones, Howie."

"Don't need to."

I would have asked him why, but at that moment a creaking noise intruded on our conversation. It sounded like a window being opened, gently, upstairs. Joelle started, dropped her beer can, and stood. She whispered, "Her window was shut."

Sam tried to say, "It's just the wind," but he wasn't convincing, not to any of us, not even to himself.

Joelle shivered. She said, "We've got to check," and headed for the stairs. As she passed the sink, she reached into a drawer and grabbed a heavy carving knife.

I had a sour taste in the back of my mouth. Still, I followed her. We all did, each of us careful not to step in the beer Joelle had spilled. Up the stairs. Down the hall. Lights on. We didn't run. We moved slowly, quietly, as if unwilling to face a truth, or like children trying not to disturb their elders.

It wasn't long before we were gathered before the closed door of Chrissy's room. Joelle was in front, her hands clenched around the handle of her raised knife. Sam eased her aside with a soft "Let me."

The door opened noiselessly. The light from the hall drifted in, augmenting the glow of Chrissy's nightlight. I could see the bed. It didn't look right. But even as I gasped, Sam was flying to his daughter. As he began to claw at the mass of blankets and — and something else — that covered the child, his wife hacked at the window sill.

I backed off, my gorge rising. Howie was staring into the room, fascinated. Chrissy's pale head was free now, but her body was still covered. With tendrils. I could make them out now. Long, twisting, branching worms, the color of twigs stripped of their bark. They pulsated. My eyes tried to follow their curves and motions. They spread out to cover the bed, diverging from a common stem. A stem that looked remarkably like a tree limb where it crossed the sill, where Joelle was chapping it in two, where blood — blood! — was leaking onto the paint. Fragments of barky dirt littered the sill.

No wonder the rash, the anemia, the nightmares, the listlessness, even the dirt they had blamed on Chrissy. But they had moved the child. How could the tree reach so far around the house? How. . . ?

There were answers, but there were no answers. Joelle finally made it through the limb. The stub snapped out the window. The tendrils lost their grip, and Sam finally stripped the last of them from their daughter. Chrissy awoke, saw, and screamed. Her parents grabbed her, lifted her, held her between them, enfolded in four arms of safety. She quieted. Sam said, "We'll go over to Paul's."

"I'll call," I said.

"Get some liquids into her," said Howie. "Beef broth's best."

My mother would have called for chicken soup, but I said nothing. I felt embarassed, an interloper in a very private scene. Howie and I headed downstairs, toward the phone and the kitchen.

We met again the next afternoon. Sam and Paul and Howie and I. The women and children were at the Johnsons'. Sam had Paul's chainsaw. He was going to cut the tree down.

We looked at the tree. Almost as one, we ran our eyes from ground to crown, up the fissured trunk, over the graceful branches and green leaves, and back. We spotted the stub left by last night's work. It was a long ways from the guest room window. I shuddered. Howie said, "Where do you want it to fall?"

"Across the yard," said Sam. "The hell with the hedge."

"Then. . . ." Howie showed him where to make the first cut.

"I know how to use a saw. Though it has been awhile." Sam hefted the machine in his hands. I could see the marks of the file where Paul had sharpened the chain. My nose caught the bite of the gas and oil he had fed it. The cans sat on the walk.

Sam took a breath. He flipped the switch. He grasped the cord. "Here goes," he muttered. He yanked. The saw came to life with a roar and a puff of smoke.

He approached the tree. He spread his legs, bent, and swept the saw toward his target. But he hardly scarred the bark. Even as the chain touched, the tree *shrugged.* There was no other word for it. The bark rippled as a wave passed up the trunk. The saw bucked. It twisted in Sam's hands, and before he could bring it under control again it sank into his left leg. He screamed.

The rest of us stood paralyzed while Sam's blood spurted from severed arteries. The tree was still. Sam screamed again. Howie grabbed my shoulder. "Harry. Your belt." I took it off. He knelt beside Sam and used it for a tourniquet. Then he said, "Paul. Call the ambulance."

When Sam was gone, Howie stood silent, staring at the tree once more. Finally, he said, "It'll take fire. But the house'll go too." He looked around. "Think Sam'll mind?"

Paul shook his head. I laughed, grimly.

"Then I'll fetch a load of firewood. Might as well take the saw home. Leave the gas, though."

Paul nodded, picked up his equipment, and set off down the walk. His head was bowed, his pace slow. I didn't envy him the task of telling Joelle what had happened. Though she must have heard the screams.

Howie said, "Better get humpin'," and took off. I remained for a moment more, thinking. The tree. What was it? What the *hell* was it? A bloodsucker, a vampire, feeding on the folks in this house for centuries. A horror from the grimiest pages of the past. Yet it looked like nothing more — or less — than a tree. Brown bark and white wood and green leaves. A promise of summer shade and shelter from the rain. When my skin crawled, I turned and left as well.

I went back to the office. Bonny was there, typing, her ankles crossed beneath her desk, her fingers flying, her eyes scanning a notepad. When I came in, she looked up and told me, "Liz found Carter's diary." She pointed at the typewriter. "You'll be interested."

"Won't help," I said. I crossed the room to help myself to her coffee. I told her what happened.

"Aiee." She grimaced. "Maybe it won't help, but wait'll I get this report done."

I nodded and took the coffee back into my office. Old diaries. What good could they do? We had a monster on our hands. We needed the auto-da-fe'."

I didn't bother to turn on the lights, even though it was growing dusky outside. I sat, sipped the coffee, and ruminated. I hoped the fire would work. The saw hadn't.

When my cup was empty, I rose to leave. As I passed Bonny, she held up the papers she had been typing. I took them, said "Thanks," folded them once, and stuck them in my jacket pocket. I ignored Bonny's disappointed expression. There would be time enough for reading later. Right now, I wanted to see how Howie was coming along.

When I reached the Dobson house, Howie was just beginning to unload the wood. I helped, and soon we had a pile of firewood, cut to size and split small, three feet high and two wide stretching from the tree to the front door. We piled the wood higher and wider right around the tree. The can of gas for the chainsaw we set, cap off, on the end of the woodpile nearer the door. Then we went inside and laid a fire in the fireplace. We laid it so it would roar.

Then we headed for the Johnsons'. We found Joelle there, already back from the hospital. "He'll be all right," she told us. "They even think they can save the leg."

"You mind burning the house?" I hoped Paul had told her.

She shook her head wildly. "No. No! Anything! Even if it wasn't insured!"

I had figured it was. That was why we had laid the fire. Make it look like an accident. "Then you'd better get a few things out first. Papers, pictures, silver, favorite books and toys and such. Just leave enough to convince the insurance folks."

She agreed. She'd do it after supper. Though there wasn't that much she couldn't stand to lose, under the circumstances. Her husband, her child. What else mattered?

Come full dark, when the streets were quiet and the children were in bed, we went back to the house, started the fire in the fireplace, helped Joelle gather what she wanted to save, and arranged the furniture to lead the fire toward the door. We opened windows to take advantage of a light breeze from the back of the house. Last of all, we raked the fire out onto the rug and left.

It went just as we had hoped. Within twenty minutes, flames were shooting out the front door like a dragon's breath. The gas can went up with a whoosh. The woodpile caught. The flames moved steadily toward the tree. It caught, and we all felt a sense of screaming.

When the fire department arrived, I held them off till I was sure the tree was dead. As Mayor, I could get away with that. Not for long, but long enough. It helped that they then concentrated on the house, leaving the woodpile and tree for last.

Eventually, I remembered the papers Bonny had given me. I took them out of my pocket, unfolded them, and began to read by the light of the dying fire. I didn't get far, though, before I beckoned Howie over. Together, then, we read, while Joelle and the Johnsons huddled, watching the flames.

Tolman Carter's diary, according to Bonny, was a detailed account of the man's preparations for the trip to the Colonies and of his life there, of his daily labors, his successes and failures, even the doings of the small community of the time. Of particular interest to us were two passages, one from the preparation stage. Carter had written: "Clothing, seed, tools, and provisions being laid by, I bethought me of the future and asked of myself of what I would most feel the lack far from England. The answer is England herself, and what speaks England to my heart is her great oaks. I therefore sought that nearby grove, reputed to be sacred to our ancestors, and gathered a single acorn that I might sow it wherever I might one day make my home."

Later, Carter had written: "Planted my oak, that my children and theirs after them may enjoy the shade of England. Already it shows a goodly sprig."

I looked at Howie. He looked at me. He nodded. "A druid oak."

I had read of the wicker cages and the fires. Had the druids sacrificed to oaks? Or to trees like this? Had the sacrifices been meant, perhaps, to keep the things quiet? To keep them from plaguing the folk around them?

My attention shifted as the roof of the house fell in with a rush of sparks and smoke. I turned my gaze to the tree. Its leaves were jewels of flame. More flames crawled along its limbs and leaped from branch to branch. Smoke and steam billowed. And from the reddened clouds, a burst of tendrils writhed toward me.

I ducked.

Downeast Encounter

The tiny flying saucer whipped past overhead. It was surely, thought Howie Wyman, the dodgamnedest trout fly ever made. It was a sliver of wood painted silver, with a row of black squares around the rim and three streaks of red artistically placed to suggest a spinning motion. It was mated to a fishhook and adorned with a hackle and three fibers from a pheasant tail feather. Just what the folks downriver had sworn they saw last summer. The same folks who swore they caught trout on churchkeys, pop-top tabs, and old cigarette butts. Hah! He'd show them, he would.

He spat a stream of tobacco juice onto the bank and pumped the rod again, letting out another fifteen feet of fly line. His weathered face was intent, on the task. Of average height, he'd once been told by his Aunt Babe that there was Indian blood in the family. He looked it. He had high cheekbones, and his hair had once been jet black, though now it was well salted with white. His fingers, so long and deft as they handled the loops of line, were gnarled. The joints swelled like the pellets in a rabbit's gut. They pained him from time to time — though not now, not in spring, not when fishing — but he took that as natural enough. He'd worked hard all his life, and outdoors at that, in the cold and wet. He was a blueberry picker. In season, that is. The rest of the year, he might do a little clamming, up to his knees in tide-flat muck. He might work in the woods a bit or help out with a neighbor's haying. He might even poach a deer or two. But all these activities were secondary. They merely kept his body and soul together, and his wife from leaving him, while he devoted all the time he could to his true love — trout fishing. Not just any trout, either. He might accept a brownie or a rainbow if it chose to commit suicide in his creel, but he wet his line only in waters he thought might hold a brookie or two.

Like here. A wide, deep pool, shaded by a wall of ledge and its crown of greening birch, fed by a spring-fast stream. Foam around the rocks at his feet. A cool, moist breeze. A glimpse of mink or deer. And every year, the trout. The speckled, leaping brook trout. The biggest he'd ever taken here had been two and a half pounds.

Spring and a trout stream! Howie was no poet, but he came close at moments like these. The great tragedy of his life was winter. Not only was the trout season closed then, thanks to the busybodies up to Augusta. but the streams were all iced in. He couldn't even poach. He had to console himself with his flies, turning feathers and hair and.bits of tinsel into barbed impressions of minnows and bugs. Even of flying saucers, he chuckled as he let his line float down onto the water's surface. The saucer touched with a gentle plop and sat there, rocking.

Emma hadn't thought much of it. "You are crazy!" she had screamed when he had produced the saucer.

"Now, now." He had waved the new fly placatingly. That had been a mistake. His wife, a tiny, forceful blonde, had needed no reminding of how her husband wasted his time. Shrilly, she had screamed again. "You're crazy! That thing won't catch fish!"

"Of course it won't. That's the whole. . . ."

She hadn't let him finish. "The car needs a new transmission! We need wood! We need clothes! Look at you!" She had pointed scornfully at his frayed denims and her own faded Sears skirt. "We need food! And you! You're busy trying to prove some *thing* to those bums you hang around with all the time!"

He had shouted her down. "It's not pointless! They say a trout'll bite on anything. I'm gonna prove it won't."

"A saucer fly!" She had laughed. "Hah! Give it to your sister's kid Petie. He'd have some fun with it. Maybe it'd help him learn to cast. Why you can't use worms and get more fish. . . ."

"I get my limit," he had interrupted hastily. He did, too. He was good, and he knew where the fish were.

"And that's damn few fish these days. Why don't you catch bass and perch and bullheads, too?"

He had shuddered. Trash fish? They might nourish his belly, but his spirit would starve. He'd have to be awful hard up, he knew, and even then his heart wouldn't be in it.

He twitched his rod tip, lifting the line and the saucer from the water. He drew back his arm, letting line and fly whip overhead into his backcast. Forward again, and back, while the hackle dried, and forward once more, to land in the lee of a boulder. He had taken trout right there before, and if a flying saucer could seem like trout food, that was the spot. But nothing happened. He flicked the line to make the saucer bob. Still nothing. Just as he had thought. They *won't* take just anything. He picked another spot, where the water flowed under the wall of ledge. He cast again, telling himself he really ought to put on a real fly and catch some dinner.

But just as his tiny saucer was settling to its landing, the water exploded beneath it. Damn! he thought. The line tautened. His rod protested as the tension overcame the drag. His rod bowed, end the fish leaped clear of the water, striving mightily to shake free the hook. It was a big one! Five pounds, if it was an ounce! The biggest he'd ever had on his line!

Twenty minutes later, he eased his net under the exhausted fish and lifted it from the water. The saucer hung from its lip like a vagrant's cigarette. The gills fluttered. The spots gleamed red and blue and gold in the sun. It was a thick-bodied spring feast for Howie and Emma. It was surely the biggest, the brightest, the best of all the trout in Maine, even if it did prove Howie wrong about his saucer.

"Please, would you take the hook out of my jaw?"

That was how it all began, early one Saturday morning. A talking trout, and a flabbergasted fisherman. I was around the bend fishing another pool, when I heard the flabbering start. Since I hadn't been having much luck, and I was about to move on anyway, I didn't hesitate. I reeled in my worm, caught the hook on the bail of my reel, and headed upstream.

It sounded interesting. A vaguely familiar male voice going "Bu-bu-bu-bu . . ." at the top of its lungs. I wondered what he'd caught, but I didn't waste time trying to guess. I needed all my attention for the rocks I was stumbling over and, besides, I'd be there soon.

In another moment, there was only a moderately large boulder between me and where the voice had come from. I rounded it and stopped. A man was squatting beside the water. His beat-up fly rod lay on a rock nearby. He was dressed in faded denim overalls; a blue work shirt, and ankle boots. The back of his neck was dark and seamed, like his boot leather. The hair that escaped the band of his crumpled green felt hat was shaggy and gray.

Even from this view, I recognized Howie, and now the flabbering struck me as a peculiar thing to hear. He had the reputation in town of being as laconic as a proverb. I stepped closer, until I saw his net and its burden. I whistled. "That's a nice one, Howie."

He looked up, startled. "Morning, Mayor. 'Tis, ain't it?"

In our small town, I had the smallest, most unpaid job. I could afford it, since I was also the local oil dealer, and it meant everyone knew me. They even, to some extent, looked to me for leadership. "Ayuh. You sounded pretty surprised when you netted it."

Howie sat back on his heels. He pursed his lips, and a gob of used tobacco hit the stream. "Well, I'll tell you. As soon as I got him beached, he suggested I take the hook out of his mouth." He reached to one side, searched with his fingers for a second, held up his fly. "This one." His eyes never left mine.

I looked. I grinned. "You sure you're not turning into one of those UFO nuts, Howie? That fly, and a talking trout?" I shook my head, still grinning. And this was the town's odd-job man. I'd have been less surprised to find Lydia Seltzer involved in a thing like this. She was the high school science teacher, and she'd nearly been fired over the wendigo business. "Ought to get you on Johnny Carson, anyway."

"He's not lying, mister." I started. The fish! Tangled in the net, on its side in a puddle between two rocks, it had squirmed itself around to face me. Its jaws were half open, its flanks heaving with effort. "Though he never would have seen me if he hadn't waved that damned *spruleer* over my nose!"

I dumped my first thought right away. Howie, a ventriloquist? And spruleer? Was that what a talking fish called a flying saucer? It *could* talk, by damn! This was something new, something I'd never thought to see. Or was I dreaming? Maybe I'd fallen and knocked myself out on a rock. My fingers trembled as I pulled my tobacco pouch out of my hip pocket and began to load my pipe. "What were you planning to do with it, Howie?"

"What the hell can you do with a fish, Mayor?" He stared at the trout, fingering his fly. He shrugged. "Even a talking one. Thought me and Emma'd have it for supper."

"But. . . ."

"Now wait a minute! I didn't come, all this way to. . . ."

"What d'ya mean?" put in Howie. "You musta hatched within a mile of here."

"I wasn't hatched!"

"So where did you come from?" I asked. "Out of a cocoon?"

The trout snapped its mouth shut as it squirmed to bring its left eye to bear on me. I might have been a bug, or another spruleer. "Close! I crashed, a year ago, and the bioformer kicked me out like this. There wasn't enough power to give me a more useful body, like a human or a bear."

"You crashed? In what? A flying saucer?"

"You got it. I was a spruleer pilot." There wasn't really anything you could call an expression on the thing's face. A fish just doesn't have the muscles. But its voice did show some kind of feeling. Pride, now, maybe. But it was hard to believe, and I couldn't resist the urge to heckle. This trout was talkative enough, but I wanted to learn all I could before I woke up. Or whatever. "In a body like that?" I said. "No hands, no. . . ."

"I told you I was bioformed! It's regulations on an inhabited world. No one leaves the ship in an incompatible shape. The computer sees to it."

"And the ship? Where's the wreck?"

"Regulations. Automatic destruct."

"You've got so many answers, it's hard to believe you. In fact, I'm not sure I do." I finally got my pipe lit. I gave it a couple of puffs to get it drawing well, and then I blew a cloud of smoke at the fish. He didn't like it. He flopped, splashing water with his tail. "Any trouble, and you're marooned, just like that. And no way to holler for help. Or is there a way?"

Well, that did it. There's nothing like skepticism to get you told, and told good. There was a way, all right, but it hadn't been working. It hinged, he told us, on the one device that never went up with the ship. Every officer had one implanted in his brain. It was a contiguity manipulator. The universe was a sheaf of world lines — of parallel worlds, to us — and with his gimmick our trout could replace any object in this world with its counterpart in another. Since in an infinite sheaf anything must exist at every point, he could in principle have anything he wanted. He could switch a boulder for a Cadillac or a cave for a mansion. But that was only in principle. In fact, he was limited by probability and energy. The most probable counterparts, the ones found in the greatest number of world-lines in some form or other, were those nearest in the sheaf to our own line. And going beyond those world-lines took more energy than his small body could supply the manipulator.

As for getting him rescued, every time he pulled a switch, he generated an improbability wave that could be detected by offworld monitors. If the disturbance was great enough, if the switch was between world-lines far enough apart in the sheaf or if it meant a large enough disruption of local probabilities, they would come and check. The trouble was, there wasn't much a trout could do in his stream to make waves. He could turn pebbles into caddis flies and twigs into minnows. It kept him well fed — he had gained three pounds in the last year — but that was about it. The really significant, wave-making alternate realities just weren't within his reach. He was frustrated, naturally, and that's why he'd struck at Howie's fly.

He demonstrated his talent by switching Howie's rod for an almost new split-bamboo rig. I didn't understand, but the rod was a beaut and it set me thinking. I was the mayor, wasn't I? I had responsibilities, didn't I? "Howie," I said. "Have you got a bucket in your car?"

"Ayuh," he answered. "But it leaks."

That wouldn't do. I looked around the rocky bank of the stream until I spotted an abandoned beer can. I retrieved it and set it down by the trout. "Can you switch that for a bucket?"

"Sure." And it was done. I had a yellow plastic pail just like the one my ex-wife once used to wash her sweaters. I filled it from the stream, and then I dumped the trout out of Howie's net into the bucket. He hit with a splash and swirled to poke his nose out of the water. "What do you, have in mind?" he asked me.

"Well," I said. "As long as you're here, you're stuck. Right? You can't change anything important enough to get yourself noticed and rescued. But we can take you someplace else, where you can shake things up a bit. Give you a chance to get home." I blew another puff of smoke in the fish's general direction and looked at Howie. I could see his thought: "There goes my dinner." I said, "Proof of the pudding, eh?"

As Howie nodded, the fish swirled again. Alien or no, he acted like a trout. His swirls were so much like the ones a real trout would make picking off nymphs that I was tempted to try a worm on him. But then his nose came up, and he said, "I was warned about this. You want me to make you rich." He sounded suspicious.

I shook my head. "Not a bit of it. It's just that I could use a little help with my job."

"Uh-huh. Just so you get me home." He didn't sound like he believed me.

"By the way, though, what should we call you?"

He cocked an eye at me, then at Howie. "What's the difference? You need a tag to remember a talking trout?"

"Then you're Oscar." Howie surprised me. Oscar? He must have noticed my expression, though, for he then turned to me and added, "Had a goldfish named that once."

"Fine," I said. "Let's get back to the cars. I'll meet you at the high school."

The town didn't have much money. Neither did the county nor, for that matter, the whole state. We'd been enjoying our own private recession for over two hundred years now, and the place showed it. Most of the roads had more cracks and potholes than pavement. The town hall needed a coat of paint, new wiring, a new roof, and God knew what else. The fire department needed new trucks; hell, it needed working trucks. The jail needed rebuilding. And the schools — well, federal money had given us a new elementary school just a few years ago, but the high school was another matter. The roof leaked. The furnace didn't work. The windows were broken. There wasn't any gym, and the athletic field was a mudflat.

When we pulled into the dusty parking lot, I waited for Howie to walk up beside my car. Then I hauled the bucket off the front seat and set it down in the dirt. "All right, Oscar," I said. "Can you see this mess? Can you switch it for a better model?"

He poked his nose out of the water and said, "Not from here, I can't. You'll have to carry me around and show me what you want replaced."

"Give us a paved parking lot."

And he did. One moment we were ankle deep in dirt. The next we were standing on nice smooth blacktop. "That was easy," said the fish. "It should give the monitors a blip, too."

Easy, he said. And I didn't have the vaguest idea of how he managed it. A fishing rod was one thing. So was a bucket. But this! A 200 by 30 strip of tar, materialized out of nothing. I consoled myself with the thought that I didn't have to understand it to take advantage of it, and we got on with the job.

I showed Oscar the playing field, the rickety bleachers, the leaky roof, the broken windows, the dead furnace, and all the rest. And as fast as he saw the problem, it was gone. In an hour, we had a brand new high school,, and it hadn't cost the town a cent. Though that wouldn't stop the hooraw come Monday morning.

I gave Howie the bucket then, and we visited the jail, the fire department, and the town hall. I got the people out of the way, gave them a little pep talk about how things were going to improve real soon now, while Oscar did his stuff, and then we ducked. I didn't want to be around when they noticed the changes.

With the town taken care of, Howie and I headed over to his place. We dropped his car there. Howie jumped into mine, and we sat there. What now? There had to be something else we could do with our pet miracle-worker, but what? I was gripping the wheel with both hands, staring thoughtfully out of the windshield, when Howie nudged me. "Say, Mayor. You've fixed up the town, but what about us? Look at my house."

I looked. It was a small frame, painted white a long time ago. The roof sagged, the windows were still covered with their winter coat of plastic, and the yard was littered with discarded junk. I thought I recognized an armchair my wife had consigned to the dump two summers ago. Without a word I lifted the bucket to my lap, let the trout get a good look too, and

Howie had a trim brick ranch with a two-car garage and a slate walk. He shook his head. "What will Emma say?" He shook his head again. I could just imagine his thoughts. But he surprised me again. He said, "And you?"

I started to say that I had enough already. I'd just been doing my job, after all. But then I stopped. I was an oil dealer, wasn't I? And I had three empty 50,000 gallon tanks, didn't I? Thanks to the allotments they laid on in '87. I stepped on the gas, and we headed for my lot outside town. On the way, I had another thought. How about the roads? Could Oscar do anything about them? I told Howie to hold the bucket up, and the potholes started filling in fifty feet in front of the car. It was the smoothest ride I'd had in years.

Once my tanks were full, we just drove, fixing up the pavement as we traveled. We hit the town's main street, twisted in and out through the residential sections, and smoothed out the three county roads that linked us up with the rest of the state. We even paved a few roads that had been dirt as long as I could remember.

It didn't take long. Three hours later, we were parking in my driveway. And we hadn't attracted any attention to speak of, even though we had met some traffic. Think about it: you're tooling along a rough road when the pavement suddenly turns smooth. Do you notice the car coming your way at just that moment, much less blame the change on it? Do you realize the new paving is approaching you a bit faster than it should? Of course not. You're too busy being grateful the sons-of-guns have finally gotten around to fixing things up.

Anyway, we were done. And if our alien trout's monitors couldn't get a fix on him from all the blips we'd made, I'd get him an upholstered aquarium with a waterproof TV. "C'mon, Howie," I said. "Let's have a drink."

He was agreeable, and as soon as I'd filled the sink with water — I have a well, so it's not treated — and given Oscar a little fin room, I got out the jug and the sandwich fixings. We settled down right there beside the sink and ate. And drank. Along the way, we found out the trout liked bologna, especially if one of us had dipped it first in his whiskey glass. That started us laughing until we both swore we'd have to try the combination out as bait. And that led Howie into telling me how he'd come to make his saucer fly.

"But you know," I said. "A trout will bite on anything."

"Horseshit," said Howie. "I know better."

"Sure. Anyway, anything that flashes just right in the water, so it looks like a minnow. Or anything that sits just right on top of the water. You take a look at one of those flies of yours sometime. They don't really look much like bugs, do they? It's the hackle. It makes dimples in the water, like legs. That's what they see. That's what they strike at."

"So how come some flies don't work?"

I shrugged. "There are folks who swear by any fly you can name." We had another drink, and Howie sloshed a bit of the bourbon into the sink. Oscar seemed to like that. He splashed his tail and heaved his gills a couple of times. And then he stuck his head up to tell us. "Nuts," he said. "Half the time it's just that we get pissed at all that crap being dragged over our heads. If we had sense enough to keep our mouths shut, you'd never catch one of us."

"Us?" said Howie.

I swear that trout seemed to snarl. His gills flared and his jaw twisted, and he muttered something about having been stuck in this body too long. He was identifying with it, and if he didn't get rescued pretty damn quick, he'd go native all the way.

I stuck my oar in by asking how long it should take. "We made enough waves, didn't we? They know you're here by now."

"Oh, they know. They're probably frantic, the things you had me doing. But they've got to zero in, and for that they'll need a few more blips."

"So keep the jug full." And it was full. "But why should they be frantic?" And then I got it. Sometimes I catch on fast. Sometimes I don't, like now. But if I had, the town would still be a shabby mess and Oscar would still be a castaway. "Hey,

"Howie," I said. "Where do you suppose all that stuff came from?"

"How should I know?" he said. He took a swig of whiskey and shrugged. "He waves a fin, and I've got a new house, or a new rod. Looked like magic the first time he did it. Still does."

Bless him! Magic! But Oscar had said something about parallel worlds. Worlds full of people just like us, people who had worked their butts off to get things we'd gone and swiped out from under them. I felt low, and I said as much. "Howie, we're no better than crooks. We stole all that stuff, and we should give it back before we're caught."

"Mayor, Mayor," said Howie. "That's gotta be the booze talking. Who's gonna catch us?"

There was a swirl in the sink. "The monitors," said Oscar. "They rescue me, ask me what I switched to make all those blips, and put everything back where it was."

"Oh, yeah," said Howie. "I like that rod." And he grabbed the jug and poured about half of it into the sink. There was a flurry of splashing as Oscar soaked the alcohol up through his gills, and then nothing but quiet. I stood to peer into the water. I wasn't any too steady on my feet, but I could make out Oscar laying on the bottom, on his side. His gills were moving slowly.

"He's out cold," I said.

"Serve him right," said Howie. "Maybe he'll wake up like me after a three-day bender."

"How's that?"

"He'll be a blank on the last week. We'll keep it all. Have another drink." I did. So did he.

In the morning, I had a head like a sack of w*et concrete. I was so thick and fuzzy that it took me half an hour to realize I wasn't in my comfortable bed, but slumped on a kitchen stool. The blur a few feet away was Howie Wyman. I kicked him, but not hard. I couldn't have dented a pillow. When he opened his eyes, I asked him, "What you doin' here?"

"We was drinking," he got out after a minute. "Coffee?"

I stumbled to my feet and found the pot. I went to the sink to fill it, did so, and set it on the range. Then I turned back to the sink. There was something about it. It was empty! My head cleared a bit. "Oscar's gone," I said.

"Oscar?" mumbled Howie. "Oh, yeah. Gone?" He got up to look, and we both headed for the living room window. The road was still smooth. We looked at each other. I pointed. "The telephone's back in the kitchen."

I got out the instant while Howie dialed his number. Emma answered. I could hear her across the room, a buzzing scream that made me pity Howie's ears. "What did you do with our house? Where have you been all night? The house!"

Howie's grin was no more relieved than my own. I reached for the bottle — it was still full, even though I knew we had kept on drinking after Oscar passed out — and poured a dollop in both our cups while he said,

"Fisherman's luck, honey. I got us a new one."

He hung up, the pot whistled, and I poured our cups full. When I handed him his, he raised it as if in a toast. We drank, and our heads began to clear. At least, mine did.

That was when I saw the note. It was stuck to the refrigerator door with one of those little magnets everyone has. I didn't remember putting anything there myself, so I crossed the room to look at it. It was printed in pencil, laboriously, as if the writer weren't really at home with the method or the language. It said:

> I have a headache, but thanks for everything anyway. Don't worry about losing the improvements. The monitors were able to compensate by drawing on one of the dead lines.

So we got to keep the goodies. I knew that already, from the window end the phone, but it was nice to know the aliens didn't balk at handing out rewards. Or should I call it a salvage fee? That trout body was equipment of a sort, wasn't it? But the note went on, and in a vein that made me laugh. I handed it to Howie and said, "It looks like one of us is going to have to get a guide's license."

He drained his cup and said, "Got one. Not much call for guides anymore, though."

But there will be. The note's last words were:

> It'll be good to see home again, but I will be back. I never did get to go fishing.
>
> — Oscar.

Protection Racket

I'm not much of a gardener. No time. I raise a few tomatoes and strawberries, salad stuff and peas and beans in the backyard. But I don't depend on them the way many folks around here do. That's why I didn't get too upset when that late frost hit and wiped the garden out. I just wrote it off with a furtive sense of relief that I wouldn't have to do all that weeding this year.

But the relief only lasted a month. By then the Fourth was over, with its parade and fireworks display and municipal picnic in the park. The mess was cleaned up, and I was in the office for my Monday afternoon stint at official business. My secretary was standing in front of my desk, telling me what my appointments were. I liked to look at her. Bonny Clark was a tall girl, dark-haired, comfortably curved, with a mouth that looked like a ripe plum tastes. I liked to listen to her, too. Her voice was soft, but not too sweet, like a good moselle. I often wished our local accent made such voices possible. Bonny had come to town from out of state, another of our in-migrants, not long before my divorce.

She was saying, "I set it up for the delegation first."

"What delegation?" I said around my pipe. This was new. I hadn't thought there was any current issue that deserved that kind of an approach to the Mayor.

She consulted her notebook. "Mr. Andrews from the greenhouse, Mr. Morse from the Maine Woodsman's Association, and Mrs. Henley for the garages. They'll be here in ten minutes."

I knew them all, though I couldn't guess what they wanted. A businessman, a woodcutter, and a bookkeeper. I didn't imagine it could be anything very crucial. I couldn't imagine how wrong I was.

Bonny went through the rest of the schedule and we chatted briefly about the weekend. Then we heard noises in the outer office. She left me and, a moment later, ushered in the delegation. Bob Andrews wore a denim jacket over a tie and a striped shirt. de was in his thirties, with short hair and a mustache that might have been engraved on his upper lip, it was that delicate. Frank Morse, fiftyish, wore a suit instead of his usual overalls. He was burly with the muscle that comes only from wrestling logs and logging machinery. Marion Henley, just entering middle age, would have looked good if she didn't spend so much time at the desk in her husband's garage. She was spreading, and her flowered dress wasn't loose enough to hide it. She was no Bonny, though there had been a time. . . .

All three looked determinedly anxious. At the same time, they seemed resolved that something be done. Their lips were tight, their eyes narrowed, their backs stiff. They refused the chairs I waved them to, and Marion said, "Mayor Bowen. Are you aware of what's been going on in this town?"

"Usually, Marion." I set my pipe down and gestured again toward the chairs. They ignored me. "But perhaps you'd better tell me what's got you so warm under the collar.

"Hmmph!" she snorted. Was she their spokesman? It seemed so. The other two were making no move to speak, leaving it to her, either by default or agreement. I couldn't tell which. "It's that Jaeckel creature. He's going to ruin this town!"

I let my eyebrows rise. The name seemed familiar, but I thought that if he was such a threat I would know more about him. "Go on."

"He came to town last winter. . . ."

"February," said Frank Morse.

"And right away he came to us and said he wanted a tenth of all the money we took in from repairing pothole damage. Called it a tithe, he did!"

"Did you agree?"

"Of course not!" She stared at the floor for a minute "But then none of the machines would work. Not even the cash register! And he said they'd be okay as soon as we decided to go along with him."

"So you did, and everything worked again." She nodded, reluctantly. I looked at the other two. "And the same

sort of thing happened with you?" It had. Mister Jaeckel — or not "Mister"; he insisted he be called "Master" Jaeckel — had gone to each of them too. At the greenhouse, be had asked for a tithe on all the seedling business they did after the first of June. Furthermore, he had promised a big boost in that business if the greenhouse would just follow his instructions: have plenty of seedlings ready for the middle of that month. He had then waved a hand, and every plant in the greenhouse wilted; they recovered when Bob agreed. With the MWA local, he had asked for a tithe on all pulpwood sales above last year's level. He had convinced them by hexing the chainsaws.

"And we had more potholes than ever," I mused. "Worse ones too. And that late freeze. The fire in the pulp yard. He seems good for business."

"But he's a witch!" cried Marion. "A wizard, if anything," I said. "Witches are women."

"I don't care what you call him," said Bob Andrews. "He says he's a marketing consultant. We say he's dangerous. Now he wants a slice of our bouquet business.

Says the men in town are going to be forgetting their anniversaries and such, and we'll be selling more."

"He told us if we paid him more the saws wouldn't need sharpening and the skidders wouldn't break down.

"He wants a piece of our tire sales now."

And Jaeckel could deliver. He had proved that. His threats were good, and so were his promises. He had to be a wizard. It was stretching coincidence too far to believe he wasn't.

"And we want you to get rid of him," said Marion. "At least, make him stop this protection racket of his."

"Have you tried the police? There are laws against witchcraft."

"But what good are they? The police can't do anything against a real witch. They can't even prove arson on him. That pulp fire was started by lightning. The night watchman saw it." Frank shrugged his helplessness. "If there's anyone. . . . It's gotta be you. That's why you're Mayor."

True. I had some experience with the strange, the unlikely. People liked such things in their elected officials, in our town anyway. But what could I do? I looked from one to another of the three before me. My hands were flat on the desk. I turned them over. "Well," I said. "I'll see. But first, I'll have to talk to the man."

"He has a place on High Street," said Bob Andrews.

Master Heinrich Jaeckel was tall, thin, and fine-featured. His black hair descended to a sharp widow's peak startlingly far down his forehead. Two streaks of bleached hair arose from the peak and ran back over his ears. The streaks were repeated on the black-furred brow and head of his pet monkey, with the addition of a third streak down his spine and tail. They each had a frankly satanic look. Together, they were unnerving.

I found them on the ground floor of a four-story house. The house was a large one for our town, al] gables and gingerbread, painted white and set back from a street on a large lot. It had become the Gilman place after the death of its ship-owner builder, and it had kept that name as it passed through many later hands. Along the way, it had lost its two elegant bay windows, replaced by a sheet of plate glass. Most recently, the house had sheltered a bookstore. That business had folded because there just aren't enough readers in our town. The shop had stood empty for over a year, the window's proud lettering slowly fading behind a film of dirt. Now the lettering was different: the window proclaimed my quarry's name and title.

Inside, the starkness of an empty bookstore had been replaced by a thick carpet, filing cabinets, wall shelves of massive tomes in antique leather bindings, and an ebony desk, set to catch the light from the window. The man sat behind the desk, toying with something that seemed made of leather and bone. The monkey perched on a corner of the desk, apparently absorbed in a book older and dustier than most of those on the shelves. When I entered, man and monkey both looked up from what they were doing. "Mayor Bowen," said the man. The monkey clapped its book shut and leaped to a shelf, where it slipped the book into an empty niche.

"Mister Jaeckel," I said.

"I prefer. . . ."

"I know. But 'Master' is for children."

"I am as a child in knowledge."

"I am sure, or you wouldn't be here." I was pushing it. Bluff. Sometimes it worked. Sometimes it didn't. I didn't expect it to work now. I was right.

"What do you want?" He seemed imperturbable. His features never even flickered at my challenge. The monkey was silent on its shelf, staring at me.

I sighed. "I want you to leave this town. I have had complaints about your business practices."

"I promise nothing I cannot deliver."

"I know. But what you deliver is at the expense of others."

"Isn't that always the case?"

"No bargain should be one-sided."

"My bargains are not. I offer better business, for a fee."

"But the business requires damage to others."

He shrugged. The motion was unnaturally fluid, as if he had no collar bones. "I also offer protection."

"Against your own harm."

"Perhaps." He raised one finger. A small blue flame seemed to dance on its tip. I blinked, and it was gone. "But you can do nothing, and I offer you a bargain. A tithe of the property taxes, for a guarantee that your tax base will not be diminished by fire."

I stared, amazed at his gall. Our town was small, but even so such a bargain would make him rich. Was this what he had been after all along? Or was he merely taking advantage of my presence? "No!" I said, and I turned for the door. Neither of us said another word. He had made his point. I would utter no threats that might all too easily prove empty. What could I do? I would have to think.

The thinking went on for weeks, and it got me nowhere. I could imagine no pressure that would affect a wizard such as he must be. And while I thought, he extended his grasp on the town. There was a rash of fires, leaking roofs, broken equipment, and the like. He never got his bite of the town's tax receipts, but he was soon getting just as much from our individual citizens. And they were scared. He was free to help himself in all the stores. His monkey was free, too, to grab fruit and candy, to deposit its wastes in vegetable bins and on piles of merchandise. No one dared to object. The man's power was too thoroughly known and too poorly understood.

People were beginning to talk of picking up and leaving town. Two of his neighbors had already left, tired of blackmail and fear and nights made sleepless by the blue glow that flickered from the top floor of the house next door. And that wouldn't do. If he sucked this town dry and drove its folk away, he would just move on. But the problem would not disappear. It would only be displaced, passed on to others. We had to lick it here, if that was possible at all.

It was at that point that I brought the matter up before the city council. I didn't have to explain myself. The councilors all knew, most of them too well.

"We should fight fire with fire," said Jack Hutchison. "Find a witch to chase him out." He was also on the school board, a contractor, as rational as me and as baffled.

"Where?" asked Bill Wylie. He was the oldest member of the council. He had been Mayor himself once.

"Cambridge," said Jack. He reached into his jacket pocket, took out his wallet, and extracted a clipping. "A few weeks ago, the Sunday paper." He tossed the clipping on the table.

We passed it around. The paper was glossier than newsprint, the sort of thing they use for Sunday supplements. The article concerned a coven of white witches, people who claimed they had "the Talent" and could cast spells. They were not, they said, like all the other so-called witches who wanted nothing more than to be unconventional. They were real, and they could prove it.

The vote was unanimous. We would consult the coven. We would hire a witch to exorcise our hex.

The witch arrived by bus. I was at the stop to meet her, half expecting an older woman, wrinkled and gray and ugly with years, a stereotype drawn from a thousand fairy tales. But the only passenger for out town was a young woman, short and blonde, clad in a dark blue skirt and sweater. She was slim except in the best of places, and though she seemed no more than college age, she carried her one small bag with the confidence of an experienced salesman. She scanned the street as she stepped off the bus, saw me staring at her, and came directly to me. When she was a yard away, just close enough for me to catch a whiff of her perfume, she spoke, "Mayor Bowen? I'm Cindy."

I raised my eyes to her own. They were blue. I must have looked uncertain, for she then added, "Yes, the coven sent me. If you would tell me what the situation is now, I would appreciate it. I'd like to get this chore over with. I don't like to be away from home for long."

"The car's down the block." I offered to take her bag, an overnight case covered with what seemed an unusually smooth leather, but she insisted on keeping it close to her. When we reached the car, it went on the floor between her legs. As soon as we were moving, I brought her up to date. I had told the coven the basics, of course, but a telephone was not the place for details in a matter like this.

When I was done, she said, "Where are we going?"

I had been just driving around, keeping the car moving while I talked, weaving in and out of the town's streets. At the moment, we were only a block away from "Master" Jaeckel's house. I told her so, and she said, "I would like to see that. Please."

I stopped across the street from the plate glass window with the gilt lettering: "H. Jaeckel, Marketing Consultant." By then, she had her case open on her knees. A small brazier stood in the open box, and she was sprinkling what looked like shreds of hay into it. When it was full, she took a small forked stick, like a miniature dowsing rod, from a pocket in the lid. Then she lit the hay with an ordinary butane lighter.

As the smoke rose in a thick gray cloud before her, she grasped one branch of the forked stick between thumb and forefinger of each hand and pointed the stem at the house through the cloud of smoke. She murmured a few words that I didn't catch. The stick trembled, twisted in her grip, and snapped. The odor of the smoke, at first spicy and warm, turned sour, as if someone had thrown sulfur into the brazier. Her face paled. Her eyes darkened. Her nostrils flared. And she passed out.

I got us out of there in a hurry. I wasn't sticking around where, if I wasn't dreaming, something had just gone wrong with magic. Jaeckel had powers that could blast innocent bystanders to hell and gone in any arcane spelling bee. Not that I was so innocent, but I still didn't fancy getting caught in the middle of a firefight.

We were six blocks away when the witch came to. By then the fire in the brazier had died out and the smoke had dissipated. I braked the car when I saw her move. I looked at her while she examined the broken remnants of her miniature dowsing rod, tucked them back into their pocket, disassembled the brazier, and closed the case. She stared down at her lap for a moment. Then she said, "You had better take me back to the bus station. There's another bus in an hour."

"Don't you want to try again later?" I made no move to start the car again.

"That would be useless. You saw what happened. He has potent allies. He is far more powerful than I thought, and I have no wish to die." She glanced at me as if to appeal for help, but there was nothing I could offer her. She returned her eyes to her lap. They stayed there until we were back where we had started.

As I held the car door for her, I said "Is there anyone else the coven could send?"

She looked at me again, her confidence gone, a young woman as uncertain as any other. "No. I am the strongest. There is no one else. No one on Earth. There is nothing you can do."

Nothing, hell! The witch might be useless, if she was really a witch at all, but everyone had a weakness. Everyone! There had to be a way to lick this wizard, this "Master" Jaeckel.

There had to be a way, but I couldn't think of it. And every time someone else had an idea, it backfired. The priest, Father Poulin, threw a bucket of holy water over the wizard and his pet. The monkey shrieked, but Jaeckel only smiled and the priest walked off the curb in front of a passing truck. Officer Perkins, whose sister's baby had died mysteriously, loaded his revolver with silver bullets he had cast himself. He then emptied his gun at Jaeckel's back, but the wizard only laughed and Perkins went home and cut his throat.

It didn't seem to fit. If there was one thing common to all the stories I had ever read or heard about the supernatural, it was the importance of symbols. Holy water was a panacea. Silver bullets were proof against vampires and were-wolves. Wooden stakes, too, and they might work here if we could think of some way to make the wizard lie still long enough to pound one through his chest. Solid symbols, ones that stood for light and earth and good. And then there were the abstract ones, the pentagrams that could contain summoned demons, the words and inscriptions. But all were useless to us. That seemed more than clear.

I was spending more and more time in my office, thinking, reading through the few books our town library had on the subject. There were tales of deals with the devil, of men who came out on top thanks to their skill in argument, of others who lost. Clearly, the devil was a philosopher, logical and precise. But how could you debate him if you had no way to contact him?

There was lore, too, descriptions that might have been written by some Infernal naturalist. But what good did it do to know demons sharpened their horns and tails on human bone? More to the point was their inability to use a mirror. At least, that could let one recognize the things.

I sought clues and wished for answers. Occasionally, I would spend an hour or two, late at night, perched on the porch of the empty house across the street from the old Gilman place. I watched shadows flitting behind drawn blinds and noted the blue flicker from the top story. He was casting spells, I supposed. Summoning his servants, or communing with his master. At such moments, I sensed his power, but I never lost my certainty. There had to be a way! If only I had Jaeckel's own books, those dusty tomes that lined his office. It might lie there. But there was no hope of getting at them unnoticed. There was no hope at all.

That was when Howie Wyman came into the picture. Grizzled and overalled, he could be taken for a farmer by anyone who didn't know how lazy he was. He spent what time he could fishing and hunting, and he did just enough odd jobs to keep his wife at home. He didn't talk much either, though what he said usually was worth listening to.

I was at home, nursing a scotch and listening to old jazz, when he knocked on the kitchen door. We got together from time to time, to drink and talk, so I wasn't surprised to see him. In fact, I was relieved. I needed someone to bitch at.

I let him in, once he'd spat his wad of chewing tobacco into the flower bed beside the door. I poured him a drink and led the way back to my living room. But I never got the chance to bitch. As soon as we had our butts in the easy chairs and our feet on the hassocks, he said, "Good scotch, Mayor. When you going to do somethin' about that wizard in town?"

I just sat there, my glass halfway to my lips, my mouth open. That he should complain! That he should even care! Though, come to think of it, why shouldn't he? He lived here, too, didn't he?

"Ayuh," said Howie. He sipped again and scratched the angle of his jaw. I could hear his nails rasping over stubble. "Found out about my guide's license, he did. Told me to pay up or my sports'd never get a fish or see a deer."

"What did you tell him?"

"Eh. I went along. What's a tenth of nothin', after all?" He grinned at me. "But we do gotta get rid of the man."

"I know," I said. I told him about the witch, about my studies and my futile thoughts. He nodded as I made each point, and he nodded again as I repeated my latest thought, "No hope."

"Maybe not," he said. "But let me think. Got more liquor?"

I did, and I got it for him. I refilled my own glass while I was at it. Then I sat, reloaded and lit my pipe, and watched him for all of half an hour. He didn't look thoughtful. He looked rather like a scruffy bum getting drunk on someone else's liquor. But in the end, he said, "I have a thought."

My eyes asked the question.

"You say they're logical. Like computers, maybe?"

He meant the demons. I nodded. "By all accounts."

"Any way to give 'em a puzzle they can't handle?"

I blinked, startled. "Like a riddle? The Barber of Seville?"

"That one's easy. The barber's a woman."

"But something like that?"

"Ayuh. I was thinkin' of the mirrors. They can't show a reflection, but if you could make one bounce off a mirror, then. . . ."

"Yes!" I said. And I could even see how to do it. Maybe. I poured us both more scotch and told him my idea. He nodded when I was done and said, "Sure, I can build it. The town'll buy the materials?"

"I'll give you a letter so you can charge them."

"And what about me?"

"If it doesn't work, you'll be lucky to get minimum wage. If it does, I'll double it."

It was ten days before I saw Howie again. I had just finished supper. The sun was touching the horizon, and I was watching it. But I turned away from the window when I heard a rumble in the driveway. I went to the door to look, and there was a five-ton truck loaded with what looked like several hundred feet of two-by-fours. Howie was in the cab. We met at the tailgate. "Here's your witch-trap, Mayor," said Howie. "We'll need a crew to set it up."

I examined the load. Two-by-fours, right enough. Each one was faced with a strip of mirror. the ends were cut at an angle and bored through. "I'll give Frank Morse a ring. How many you think we need?"

The answer was a shrug. Four, I guessed, and went inside to call. Frank was home, and he'd be right over. He would round up the men on the way. When I returned to the driveway, I told Howie as much, and he said, "Better get a jug out."

I did, and we passed it back and forth until Frank arrived with his four woodcutters. Then we passed it all around while I explained what we would do. "We'll set this up around Jaeckel's house," I said. "Once it's good and dark. It'll fit. He's got a big yard."

"But what is it?" asked one of the woodcutters. I hadn't caught his name.

"A witch-trap. I hope."

"How're we gonna put it together?" asked Frank.

I looked at Howie, and he stepped up to the cab of his truck, on the right. He opened the door and extracted a heavy cloth sack. "Hex bolts," he said.

I laughed. Symbols! As if they would do any good! But what else could we try? It would be dark enough soon to work unseen. In the meantime, there was the rest of the bottle.

And then it was gone, the liquor and the light both. We moved, Howie and I in the truck, Frank and his crew in his car. We crossed the town, which didn't take long, and coasted the last hundred feet, stopping around the corner from the wizard's place. We didn't want to be seen. We all remembered what had happened to Father Poulin and Officer Perkins.

It took us two hours to unload the truck — quietly, speaking only in whispers — and assemble the witch-trap. I made sure all the mirrors faced the house as we ran the two-by-fours through shrubbery and over lawn, close to the house in spots, jutting over the sidewalk in others. When we were done, the house was surrounded. I checked it one more time, murmuring words I'd memorized a week ago, and then we retired to the porch across the street.

The neighborhood was silent, as it had been when I had watched alone. There were no chirps of crickets, no bird sounds, no hint of dog or neighbor. The people were staying indoors, scared. The animals, the creatures of lawn and tree, seemed to have disappeared. "I hope he's home," I said.

"His lights are on," said the woodcutter, whose name I didn't know.

"Then I hope he doesn't decide to take a walk."

"He never does," said Frank. "Not once the sun goes down."

"We're safe, I think," said Howie. "Long as that thing works."

"And if it doesn't?" Another woodcutter.

"Then we don't care," I said. Or would we? If magic, black magic, could exist, then so could souls. And so could a hell to which we could all be dragged. I would be happy to be back in my office again, with Bonny to look at and more mundane things to worry about. My mind went on like that, silently fretting, until we saw a glimmer in a fourth floor window. It seemed that Jaeckel preferred candlelight for whatever he did there.

"Almost midnight," whispered Frank.

No one answered. We watched, holding our breaths for moments at a time. I had seen it before, of course, but the gooseflesh still ran up my spine when the first touch of blue showed in the window. It strengthened, began to flicker, and we could hear — faintly — what might have been a chant. We could make out no words. I thought that even if we could we would not recognize them.

The show went on. Our joints stiffened. We shifted our positions, scratched at sudden itches, and then we gasped. The flicker stopped. The blue light flared and went out. We heard a scream. A scream that went on and on, fading as if the screamer were slowly moving away from us. It ended in a burst of flame.

"So it worked," said Frank. His voice was still hushed, though the need for quiet seemed gone. "It worked."

"Thank God," I said. We lingered on the porch, watching the flames spread. As their light increased, we could make out two points of the star we had built that evening. The mirrors gleamed and sparked. Somewhere, not too far away, a dog barked.

"But why? What did we do?"

"He summoned a demon," I said. "Used it to do his mischief. And we turned it back on him."

"But how?"

"A demon can't bear a riddle it can't solve," I pointed. "The pentagram would have boxed it in if we had known the proper spells. As it was, I had to use the Book of Common Prayer. That may have helped." I was speaking slowly, bemused by our success, but I needed little prompting. I went on. "But the mirrors really did it. The demon saw them, but knew it could not be reflected. Since the mirrors were part of the pentagram, it bounced anyway." I paused to stare into the flames. "It was a contradiction the thing could not resolve. It became infuriated and turned on its summoner."

Another dog barked. A cricket chirped. Signs that the wizard's influence was truly gone. We left too, before the firemen arrived.

Speed Trap

This summer was something special. First off, a gang of tourist kids thought they saw a herd of deer in a field, jumped the fence, and scared the cream right out of Bob Brader's dairy cows. Then six folks swore they saw a Checker taxi take off from the little airport south of town. A squad of cops from Washington took over the town's only motel. And Bonny Clark came to me about her kid brother.

Bonny, my secretary, was competent enough to make being a part-time, unpaid Mayor easy and decorative enough to keep my mind off the drawbacks of the job. She wore her dark hair in a city cut that let her ears show, filled her clothes in a way that would make a bunko artist forget his angles, and spoke as intoxicatingly as a good Moselle. But her best feature was her face. Skin that needed little makeup, intelligent, sympathetic eyes I couldn't forget, a largish nose that nevertheless balanced the whole as nicely as could be, a mouth that made me ache to taste it. I spent a lot of time watching her.

"Any appointments today?" I asked. It was a hot day, and we hadn't been able to use the air conditioners all summer. I had just arrived at the town hall, and I was already sweating, even in my shorts and open-necked shirt. As I walked into my office, Bonny followed me. She looked cool in her thin shirtwaist.

"No, sir," she said. "Things are quiet. But . . ."

"But what?" I sat down and rummaged a pipe from my desk drawer. I filled it and lit it, watching her, noting at last the preoccupied set to her face. I blew out a cloud of smoke and added, "Something's bothering you."

She looked down at the pen and notepad in her hand. "It's my brother," she said softly.

I raised my eyebrows and gestured toward one of the chairs in the room. She sat down. I wasn't sure whether the sigh I heard then was from her or from the seat cushion. "It's been two years since I saw him," she said. "And now he's come to visit. For the summer, I guess."

"That doesn't sound so bad," I said. "But there's something else, isn't there?"

She glanced up for an instant before returning her gaze to her lap. She hesitated, began to doodle on her pad. I didn't say anything. There were no appointments; we had all afternoon. And I liked to watch her, though not so much when she was sad. Finally, she said, "He smokes dope. Marijuana. And he talks about how this summer's going to make him rich."

"He's not working?" I didn't really have to ask. The coast of Maine, seventeen hundred miles of coves and inlets, several of them just a few miles away from us, is ideal for smugglers. That was true during Prohibition, and it's true today. Now it's drugs, not booze. Yachts and small freighters packed to the gunwales with bales of grass, mostly. The Coast Guard catches many of them, but they miss so many more that Maine is now a major port of entry for the stuff. "What do you want me to do? Tell the Coast Guard?"

She shook her head, bouncing her hair around her ears. "No!" She paused to glare at me. "No. We haven't been close since we were kids, but, but he is my brother."

I understood. Stop the shipment, but keep him out of it. "I'll see what I can do," I said. "For now, though, why don't we get out of here? There's nothing going on, and the diner's a lot cooler."

She smiled at me. She stood up, and now there was more spring to her, more of the Bonny I was used to. I grinned as she disappeared out the door, on her way to freshen up. People brought me the damnedest problems. That was, I supposed, a Mayor's job, particularly in a small town. People counted on me, and once I agreed to try, they did seem to feel better.

Johnson's Diner was a hole-in-the-wall joint, small, poorly lit, and busy. Barbara specialized in organic food, which brought her the sprouts crowd, but she also laid on good coffee and better pie, which brought her the rest of us. I didn't feel like coffee just then — too hot — but she had iced tea too, and that went just as well with her coconut cream pie. Bonnie didn't want the pie.

We were at one of the narrow picnic-type tables against the wall, sipping our tea. I was asking Bonny for what she could tell me about her brother — Steve, college dropout, 25, couldn't hold a job more than a month, divorced twice, he claimed, though Bonny wasn't sure he'd ever bothered with the technicalities

— when Barbara leaned over the table, one hand on my shoulder. "Hiya, Harry. You hear what's got Jim Braun so pissed?"

"No." I shook my head. Barbara was a pleasant woman, determinedly blonde but with a patient, cheerful face. She managed to keep her weight down, too, though I knew she sampled her wares. "Not a word."

"A bunch of feds've moved into his motel. They won't tell him a thing, not even how long they're going to be there, and he has to send the bill all the way to Washington." Her eyes gleamed with suppressed laughter. "He says it'll be a year before he gets paid. At least."

"Ayuh. He's got a problem, all right." I looked at Bonny. Her lips were suddenly tight, her nose a little pale around the edges. "What do you think, Barbara? Treasury agents, maybe? The drug squad?"

She shrugged. "Who knows? I'm not even sure Jim cares, as long as they get out and let him get back to his tourists." A customer called, and she turned away, though not without her usual parting shot "Be good, Harry. Don't waste our taxes."

When she was out of earshot, I turned back to Bonny. I patted her hand where it rested beside her glass. "Looks like there's not much time to waste. They wouldn't be here unless the shipment was due soon."

She gave me a look, but it didn't last. Her gaze slid past me to the back of the restaurant, where Barbara kept a couple of those electronic space-war games. She stiffened. "There he is."

I turned to look. Only one of the machines was going. Around it were three men. Two of them were razorcut summer types in leisure suits. One was a shaggy-haired, lightly bearded, denim-clad youth. He had a gold button in the ear. "The earring?" I asked.

She nodded.

"And his friends?" I had my ideas.

She had hers too, and she didn't like them. She pushed her glass away. It was still half full. "I'm going back to the office. There is some paperwork."

I thought I'd start by sticking my nose into our local tavern, Rollie's Cafe. I might find Howie Wyman there. If not, I was sure someone in the place would know where he was. I was right.

The Cafe was just down the street from the diner, a dim room behind windows brown with flyspecks. It was cool, too, redolent with beer and whiskey and stale tobacco. The tables and chairs were rickety with age and the wear and tear of frequent brawls. The solidest piece of furniture in the room was the bar, a massive piece of mahogany whose dignity was only a little marred by its scars. The bartender. Rollie, was an ex-boxer, long gone to seed and fat but still strong enough to protect his stock. When I slipped my butt onto a stool and crooked a finger at him, he reached for the pump. I shook my head — no beer today — and he came over, wiping his hands on a dirty towel. "Nice day, Mayor."

"Ayuh. Seen Howie?"

He shook his head. A voice spoke up from the back of the room. "Gone fishin' over to the Oscar pool."

"Thanks." I got up to go, but a hand on my arm stopped me.

"Hey, Mayor." It was Andrew Fish. Tall, skinny as half a rail, a real Ichabod, he ran the lumberyard just outside town when he wasn't in Florida visiting his grandchildren. "You hear about the fuss at the airport last night?"

"Nope. What happened?"

"Some joker tanked up his car with jet fuel and took off." Andrew made one hand swoop toward the rafters. "Right up in the air."

I looked at him. He had a glass of beer in the other hand, but he didn't look like he'd been in Rollie's long. He was sober. "Sounds like Lloyd Ferris," I said.

Andrew nodded and took a swallow of his beer. "Him and his super-cars."

Christ! As if I didn't have enough to worry about with Bonny and her brother and the feds, now I'd have to get Lloyd to dismantle his latest brainstorm. Most of the time he was a mechanic. A good one, too. He took care of my car. But he had dreams, dreams of Daytona and Indianapolis, of speed and fame. And every so often he figured out a new way to soup a car. "I'll go talk to him. If you see Howie, tell him to find me."

"Glad to."

Lloyd's place was in the woods on the other side of the airport. When I pulled into the yard, I didn't see any lights in the barn he used for a shop, so I went to the door of the house. It had been a trailer once, but he'd added rooms until he had a two-story house that looked almost normal.

He opened the door before I could knock. "Mayor Bowen! Thought I'd be seeing you soon."

"Ayuh. After last night?" I followed him in and accepted the cup of coffee he poured me.

"Yeah. This time I've really got it. Remember those cars they had back in the fifties? Fantastic fins? Straight, clean, sharp, like wings, except you had to watch your ass crossing the street? They could slice it right off! Nearly got me once too!"

I remembered, and I told him so. But that didn't shut him up. The man could talk your ears off, and he would, too. He was a small man, rabbitty with buck teeth and receding chin. His eyes were close-set and his nose was large. I supposed he talked so much because he didn't get many chances. People didn't have much to do with him except on business or, like now, when he was in some trouble. He was a bachelor, of course.

"Those fins!" he said. "Did you know a couple makes'd lift right off the ground if they went too fast? One of 'em, a Chevy I think it was, was even used by the cops for awhile. But not once a few Smokies took to the woods in the middle of a chase! They hit 80 or 90, and the wheels came right off the tar!

"That's what gave me this idea." I didn't ask him what idea. I knew he'd get to it, eventually. In the meantime, I sipped his coffee and tried not to mind the stink of dirty engine oil that floated around him. "Why not do a real fin job? Scoop and flare the fenders. Put a nice sharp flange around the roofline. Smooth out the grill and lean it into the wind. Shape it all for lift, and brace it so you can hang your wheels off it in the air. And then a retractible air dam so you don't take off at 40."

I shuddered.

"Well, that's what I did. I took an old Checker, gave it a rebuilt V8 and a new suspension, and then I got out the old torch."

I set my empty cup down on the kitchen table. "And it worked?"

He shook his head. "Oh, it flew, right enough. But no control. I had to wait till I could get my hands on some of the surplus that hit the market when they closed the air base up north. Now it works. Want to see?"

I supposed I had to. I nodded, and then I followed him out to the barn. We walked in. He yanked a tarp off his creation. And there it was. Fins weren't the half of it. That old Checker had been massaged till it looked like something out of Buck Rogers. The air dam looked like a cowcatcher off an old-time locomotive, only in chrome. The fenders flared like shirt-collars. The roof looked like a hat with an eighteen-inch brim and the tail piece from a Cessna for a crown. The windows behind the driver's seat were covered with sheet metal, and sticking out of what used to be the trunk was what looked like the open mouth of a twenty-gallon garbage pail. The whole thing was painted Day-Glo orange.

"You like it?" When I couldn't speak, he only laughed. Hell, he cackled. "Everything behind my seat there is fuel tanks. I can fill 'em at the airport. Hold 300 gallons and'll keep me in the air for an hour while I blow it out that FG-111 engine."

"And it works?" was all I could say.

"Bet your ass. I could take that thing out on the highway, hold it at 80 till I've got a cop on my tail, all lights and siren and whoop-de-doo. Hit the air dam release, step on the go button, and lift right up to 500 feet. Melt his windshield with my backblast, bank over to another road. and I'm home free."

I stared. At him. At his . . . car. I thought. He had actually ridden that thing last night. Flown it, really. "More a plane than a car, isn't it?"

He nodded eagerly. "Sure It's a jet. But people'll love it when they see it on the tracks."

"If you ever get it there, Lloyd." His face fell. I almost felt sorry for him. Every time he had one of his great ideas, someone stepped on it. Usually it was me. "You keep it on the ground for now. It's a plane, and that means you need some kind of a license from the FAA."

"That's what they told me last night. But, hell, the feds don't care about what's going on out here in the woods. They've got more important stuff to meddle in."

"Sure they do. That's why there's a squad of 'em in town right now." His eyes widened. His face paled. I hastened to reassure him. "Nothing to do with you, though. Don't worry about them. Just concentrate on getting that license."

I didn't think he'd have much luck.

When I got home later that afternoon, Howie was parked in my driveway. I stopped beside him and climbed out of my bucket seat. He opened the door of his pickup and stepped down. He was dressed in his usual overalls and work boots. A floppy green felt hat was pushed to the back of his head. He hadn't shaved in two or three days, and his face had a silvery cast that matched the shaggy locks escaping his hat brim. I led the way toward the kitchen door. "Heard you went fishing," I said.

"Ayuh." He shifted his wad of chewing tobacco from one cheek to the other. He spat a dark stream onto the lawn.

"Get any?"

"No Oscars."

If anyone I knew better matched the stereotype of a State of Mainer, he concealed it well. Howie, I'd heard it said, was as laconic as a proverb. He generally spoke no more than he had to. When he did speak, though, he was usually worth listening to. Take the Oscar case, for instance. Most folks would be hashing that story over for years after the event. But not Howie. This was the first time he'd mentioned it — in my hearing, anyway — in more than a year.

"Fat chance, hey?" I said as I opened the door. When he didn't answer, added, "C'mon in. I've got a chore for you."

A few minutes later, with samples of my best scotch in our fists, I told him about Bonny's brother. I outlined the problem, told him the feds were already in town, and asked him, "Think you can get close to him? Find out what's going on? Keep him out of the mess?"

"If he likes fishin'."

"There isn't much time."

He waved his glass in the air on the way to his mouth. I shouldn't worry. So I relaxed and told him what Lloyd Ferris was up to. "That is some machine, Howie. If Lloyd has the sense God gave a rabbit, he'll patent it and make a million."

"He ain't," said Howie. "I watched him. Last night. He jist wants to go fast."

I supposed that was right. We had another drink, and Howie left. I had my supper to fix, and he had his waiting for him. And Emma wouldn't be any too pleased if he was late. She didn't care for cold food.

I spent the first part of the next morning taking care of my oil business. Making sure the bills went out on time. Trying to talk the company into increasing my allocation. Sometimes they failed to understand that it gets cold up north, that we're not greedy, that we really do need more oil than they do down in Connecticut and New York. I wasn't sure I got it through their heads this time, I would find out when the truck came, next week.

That took two hours. When I was finally free, I drove over to the town hall and went upstairs to my office. There wasn't much time. That was what I'd told Bonny, and it was what I'd said to Howie. Now I thought it might make sense to learn just how much time there wasn't.

Bonny followed me into my office. I sat down and looked at her. She was wearing a white blouse and tan slacks today, easy on the eyes as ever. But she seemed anxious, and that spoiled it, a little. I said, "Think you can find out who's the chief of that bunch from Washington?"

She nodded and made a note on her pad.

"Try to get him over here this morning, then. I want to talk to him."

She nodded again. Her lips curled upward at the corners as her face relaxed. "You want to know their plans?"

"I'm going to try, anyway."

She left the room, and I settled down to the papers in my In basket. Reports to read, forms to sign, a grant application to approve. Not too much, since our town is small, but just as important as the paperwork in any other city. I was halfway through the stack when Bonny stuck her head in the door to say, "He'll be here in twenty minutes. A Mr. Lawrence Gleeson."

So. Time enough for a cup of coffee. Time enough to empty the basket. I accomplished both, with a minute to spare. I even got my pipe lit before Bonny showed him in.

My first impression was that he looked like an engineer. He was of average height, thick-set, and clean-shaven, though he would need to meet his razor again before supper. He had soft brown eyes, and his hair was dark and curly. He looked competent, a doer, a man who would brook no nonsense from man or nature. But then I noticed his suit. It was well-cut linen, light blue, and it stamped him as government as surely as the thin folder he was holding out to me.

"Have a seat," I said as I scanned his badge. It was genuine. "Mr. Gleeson . . ."

"Call me Larry, Mayor Bowen."

"Then I'm Harry." If that was the way he wanted it, fine, but I wasn't fooled. "We've been wondering what you're up to here. A drug case?"

He smiled with everything except his eyes. "That's right. I should have come by to introduce myself right away, but you know how it is. Busy, busy."

I waved a hand vaguely. Smoke eddied in its wake. "We're just curious anyway."

"Perfectly understandable. Though I'm sure you know about the smuggling up here."

"It's in the papers all the time."

He nodded. "Of course. Nothing unusual. A schooner sailing north, with some thirty tons of dope. It'll duck in to shore some dark night, unload, and be gone before anyone notices."

"It's coming here?"

He nodded again. "That's our information. But we're being cautious. We've dealt with this bunch before. Last time, they scuttled the boat before we could board."

"And you don't want that to happen this time."

"Right. We'll try to jump them while they're too close to shore to try that stunt again."

I grinned at him. "Can't wait, can you?"

He smoothed the pants leg over one knee with a hand. "There isn't much waiting left."

"Oh? When d'you expect them to show up?" I tried to look merely curious. I didn't want him to think the answer made any difference to me. I think I succeeded.

"Another day or two. They passed Cape Cod yesterday."

Time really was short then. I hoped Howie would be able to get somewhere with Steve, Bonny's brother. I knew what was up, all right, but I still needed a way to keep Steve out of the trouble. If I didn't come up with something he was bound to walk right into the trap.

Gleeson and I made a few more noises at each other, I promised all the cooperation the town could offer, and he left. I was relieved to see him go. Dope was an ugly business, from either side of the fence. But now I had to tell Bonny how tight the schedule was.

I didn't hear anything more, from either Howie or Gleeson, for another two days. The waiting wasn't easy. Bonny kept asking me for news, and I didn't have any to give her. All I had was hope, hope that nothing was going wrong. I didn't want to see Bonny hurt, and I didn't particularly want a load of dope going through our town.

But the waiting did come to an end. Howie walked into the office just after Bonny and I had returned from the diner. He looked as disreputable as ever, but when he took a chair, I kicked the wastebasket out from under my desk so he could spit and said "Well?"

"He won't talk," said Howie.

"That part's all right." I told him what I had learned from Gleeson. "But can you keep him out of the way when the time comes?"

"He don't fish."

Sometimes Howie exasperated me. Like right now, for instance. What earthly difference did it make whether Steve Clark liked to fish or not? Was that the only excuse Howie could think of to get a man out of town? I was about to say as much when I was stopped by the phone. I grabbed at it with the faint hope that maybe now I would hear some sense.

The caller was Gleeson. Once we had the preliminaries out of the way he said, "You still interested in this case?"

"Of course I am," I said.

"Then you might come down to the dock tonight. Come along on the cutter."

"Tonight? You know their schedule?"

"We know what it looks like anyway. They're a few miles out right now, tacking round waiting for dark."

"Then I'll be there. Thanks."

I hung up. I turned back to Howie, glad that now I had something else to say. "So tonight's the night."

"'Swhat it sounded like."

"You've got to get the kid out of the way."

He shrugged. "How?"

I shrugged back at him. "How should I know? Kidnap him. Take him out in the woods and dump him. Anything, just so he doesn't give his sister any grief."

"Got an itch for her?" He grinned.

I glared. So what if I did? It wasn't anyone's business but my own, and maybe, eventually, Bonny's. But our town was too small to keep such things private. I stifled the glare. "Just keep him out of the way. I'll be with Gleeson on the cutter. I want to see how they handle it."

He went along with me and let the Bonny subject drop. "What're they gonna do?"

"Seize the boat, I guess. Grab the cargo for evidence. Though they seem worried that the crew will try to scuttle it."

"But how're they gonna stop 'em?"

"I suppose they'll board from the cutter. What else can they do?"

"Chase 'em on the rocks, maybe."

"Like how?"

"Buzz 'em with a jet."

"Lloyd?"

He nodded. "Might work."

"It might, at that," I said. "I'll look into it."

It did, too. As soon as Howie had left, I called Lloyd and put the idea to him. Did he have enough control on his rig to buzz a boat? Was he game to try it? He laughed at my questions. Was he game? Was I crazy? He'd love an excuse for a few didoes. But hadn't I told him he was grounded? I told him to can it and go get that souped-up taxi of his gassed up and ready. I'd let him know when to fly sometime tonight.

Then I called Gleeson back. I had to wait while someone fetched him out of a conference, but I had him on the line soon enough. I started right off with, "Hey, Larry. You told me this crew likes to scuttle. How are you going to stop them?"

There was a brief silence. Then he said, "We plan to let them get too close to shore for that. It won't work unless they're in deep water."

"This stretch of coast is pretty steep. They won't be far from deep water."

"I know."

"So how'd you like an ace in the hole?"

"You have one?"

"Ayuh." I told him. He was skeptical, but he finally agreed to try it if necessary. He would put a man with a walky-talky at the airport to tell Ferris to start and where to go.

So that was taken care of. I called Bonny in and told her what was up. Howie would keep her brother out of the way while I watched the roundup. And then it would be over. Steve would be safe, the dope would be stopped, and everything would go back to normal.

I stopped talking when her eyes began to glisten. She didn't seem about to cry, since she was smiling, too, but . . . "I knew you would do it," she said. She paused to wipe her eyes. "I'm sorry. Can I come along with you? I'd like to watch too. I won't be any trouble."

How could she be? But I only said, "Of course you can."

The night was almost perfect for smugglers. The full moon was almost two weeks away. The sky was overcast, the offshore wind was gentle, and the smell of rain was in the air. It was so dark that when we boarded the Coast Guard cutter about ten we couldn't have seen the boat from the dock without the lights.

Gleeson met us at the head of the gangway. He was still dressed in his fancy suit, though the men moving around the deck behind him wore more seagoing dungarees and ducks. We shook hands, and when he looked curiously at Bonny, I said, "My secretary."

He nodded and said, "All right, then. You got here just in time. We leave in ten minutes."

"Where we going?"

"Blueberry Cove. Someone's parked a tractor-trailer by the old wharf in there."

"You think that's where they're headed?"

"Where else? They have to have something to haul the dope away in." He turned away, then, to speak orders in a quiet voice. His own men and the Guardsmen jumped to obey him. The gangway was drawn in. The lines were slipped and the lights went off. The cutter's powerful engines muttered below deck. The boat slid away from the dock, which quickly vanished in the dark. We left the harbor, began to rise and fall as we met the Atlantic's swells, ran north and east for a short while, and slowed beside another shore. Gleeson came back to us just long enough to say, "The Cove is just ahead. We'll wait here."

A crewman appeared out of the dark to say, "They're on the way."

"Radar?" I asked.

Gleeson said, "Of course," and disappeared again. Bonny and I continued to stand side by side, braced against the movement of the deck. There was none of the electric nonsense of youth, but I still appreciated the occasional touch of hip or arm as we swayed. And then she said, "Harry? I don't feel like a secretary."

At night, alone on the deck of a boat at sea, together, I knew what she meant. At our next touch I let my arm slip around her waist. She leaned into me. "And I don't feel like a boss."

The mood might have taken us further, but at that moment there was a sudden flurry of soft voices. I strained to hear, made out a whispered "They're in the Cove!" and let go of Bonny. There was no noise. Our own engines were off, and the smugglers' schooner was running on sail alone, trying to escape notice in silence.

The quiet ended when the cutter roared to life. We surged ahead and swung into the Cove as a seaman fired a flare. The sudden burst of light brought noon to the scene. I could see several figures on shore, grouped around the open back of a truck. The schooner was almost at the wharf, its crew on deck, ready with mooring lines.

The scene disintegrated with the light, though. Men shouted and ran about. Sails slatted and a marine engine roared to life. The schooner turned away from shore, heading for the center of the Cove, for the narrow passage we now blocked. I heard Gleeson's voice rising above the turmoil, shouting, "Get that jet in the air!"

We bore down on the smugglers. They dodged. We changed course, and they dodged again. The schooner began to seem lower in the water, its movements sluggish. Another flare went up to replace the first, already fading. But before the new glare flooded the sky, I spotted headlights above the hill to the south. Lloyd was on the way!

Seconds more, and that garish Checker was in sight below the flare, flame and smoke thundering from its trunk. It turned above us, dove on the now-floundering schooner, swooped and rolled. Its exhaust caught a sail and burst it into flame. The smugglers dove into the sea. The ship, unattended, headed back to shore. I thought it would make it well before it sank.

But then Lloyd's jet flickered and failed. He lost altitude, lurched as the jet caught again, and fell further when it failed once more. He hit the water, the jet caught one last time, and the car began to plane, its wheels keeping it from taking the air. It picked up speed, turned past the schooner, and headed for shore. It bore down on the wharf, front end lifted well above the waves, hit it, bounced, and landed on the planks. It rolled straight toward the truck, scattering waiting smugglers, and hit. The sound of the crash seemed surprisingly small. I guess Lloyd's brakes had worked, even wet.

I felt a hand on my arm. It was Bonny. I covered it with my own, and we stood that way while Gleeson and his men collected the demoralized smugglers, loaded them into the truck, and headed it for town and the cells awaiting them. The dope would be a longer job. The schooner was safe in shallow water, but its cargo was thoroughly waterlogged by now. Still, it was evidence and it would be salvaged. But not till day.

Lloyd was intact. He had sense enough, it seemed, to wear a safety harness. He did not have sense enough to call a wreck a wreck. When Bonny and I reached shore, he was standing beside the dished-in front of his machine, contemplating the damage.

We stopped beside him and looked the situation over. The car sagged on its wheels, a sign of broken springs. Salt water dripped from every edge. The cowcatcher was intact, but the grill above it was pushed back against the radiator and engine. I doubted the car would run without a lot of work. I said, "Thanks a lot, Lloyd. That was a beautiful job. Too bad it had to end like this." I gestured at the car.

He turned to me. "What d'you mean? There's nothing wrong with this machine that I can't fix in a week or two. Gives me a chance to improve the thing, too. I've got a few ideas."

"You'd better," said Gleeson. He had come up behind us. "That was the neatest piece of business I've seen in years. And I'll say so in my report. I wouldn't be surprised if you manage to sell all you can make. They'd be great police cars!"

Lloyd had lucked out. I'd given him a perfect demonstration for a perfect market. And me? Well, maybe I'd lucked out too. Bonny was still holding onto my arm, and we hadn't seen any sign of her brother. Howie must have been successful. I turned to her and said, "I'd better take you home. It's late."

Her grip tightened briefly. "One o'clock isn't that late, is it?"

As I said before, this summer was something special. I had been a long time since I last felt as silly as I did right then. I felt even sillier when I caught Gleeson's grin.

Neither one of us was thinking of Steve when we passed Rollie's. We were on the way home — hers or mine, we hadn't said — but the tavern was all lit up, still open, and it seemed a good idea to stop for a drink.

The noise stopped us even before we opened the door. Hoots of laughter competed with anguished screeches. Bonny gasped. I remembered.

We went in, and I will never forget the sight that greeted us. Rollie was leaning on his bar, ham-like arms quivering as the tears rolled down his cheeks. Howie was leaning back in a chair, grinning like a madman. And Bonny's brother was on the floor stretched flat, one of our neighbors holding his feet, another his arms while Andrew Fish wielded the shears around his head. Steve was the one screeching. The blood on his cheek may have had something to do with it.

When Howie managed to straighten his face, he told us, "It was a struggle to pin him. Specially after that earring tore out." He pointed. There was a glint of gold on the table beside him. "Kept saying he had an appointment."

Bonny was horrified. She said. "You . . ." and let go my arm.

I said, "Not anymore, he doesn't."

At that, Steve quit struggling. "What. . . ?"

"The Coast Guard," I said.

He glared at his sister. "Goddam you!"

I don't think he figured we'd done him any favor.

Fishing Trip

I had spent the afternoon over at Goose Pond, just north of town. I had hoped to catch a glimpse of the Loch Ness Monster, but no such luck. They were there,

I knew. A round dozen of the things had been stocked three years ago, and they had been spotted since. But they were secretive beasts, and they weren't seen often. I hadn't seen a one since put-in day.

No one knew how many were there now. Presumably there were more than twelve. The pond was deep, with a rocky bottom, and it was full of Atlantic salmon and trout, perfect Monster food. Sheep, too, in nearby fields. The farmers swore up and down that the things were worse than coyotes. Their stock disappeared, and the only sign was strange gouges in the pond's banks, gouges that had never been seen before.

At the time, most folks had agreed with the Department of Fish and Wildlife that the stocking was a great idea. People knew the Loch Ness Monster was real, thanks to the dolphin searches of the '80s. When the first ones were captured, everyone wanted to see them. Then the conservationists got into the act — SAVE NESSIE! SPREAD HER AROUND! — and Loch Ness was turned into a stock farm. Every place with a suitably deep and fishy lake got its quota. Now they were all over the place, in the Great Lakes, in Champlain, Tahoe, Great Slave, Baikal, Victoria. Even in Maine, though the anglers had kept them out of Moosehead.

I supposed Nessie wasn't an endangered species anymore. I liked the thought that I had a chance to look for her, too, and right in my own backyard, at that. But people weren't so happy with the transplant project now, and as Mayor of our town I had to worry about the squawkers. The farmers who didn't like extra predators. The fishermen who resented competition for their own prey. The town cops who bitched at the crowd of rubberneckers on the road around the pond. Not that I was paid to worry. I wasn't paid at all, and sometimes I wondered why I bothered. Then I told myself that I knew the answer. People voted for me, and I was lucky at dealing with the various problems that came my way. I had a responsibility, an obligation. But I did wish there were more compensations.

I was saying as much to Howie Wyman. He was an old friend of mine, with the blessed characteristic of never saying much. I could bitch at him all day, and he would just sit there, wrapped in his perennial dirty overalls, occasionally hawking tobacco juice into his lard-can spittoon, and once an hour or thereabouts, muttering some sympathetic expletive.

We were sitting in his living room, each of us with a glass of whiskey in our fists. Usually we did our drinking at my house, but this week his wife was in New Haven, visiting a sister. When she was around, I steered clear of the place. So did Howie, for that matter. Emma was a shrew, a harridan, a nagging, screaming critic of everything her husband did or didn't do. Howie spent as much time as he could fishing or hunting. When he had to, he did odd jobs, just enough to pay the bills and keep Emma with him. I often wondered why.

When I got to the Goose Pond problem, Howie said, "Goddam dinosaurs."

"They're not dinosaurs," I told him. "They're plesiosaurs."

"Ayuh, Harry. But what difference's that make? They're still eatin' up the fish." He produced a particularly nasty splat in his makeshift spittoon and hauled a wad of tobacco out of his hip pocket. He brushed the lint off, broke it in two, and tucked the smaller piece into his cheek.

I started my pipe. It had gone out while I was talking. I retamped it and lit it again. It was hard to believe we used the same weed. "Migratories, Howie," I said. "The Nessies hardly make a dent in 'em."

"'S'what they say. Don't believe it. Gotta be twenty or thirty of the things."

And at a half a ton apiece or so, that meant a lot of trout and salmon down their gullets. And Howie liked to fish. In fact, he even had a guide's license. Put it all together, and that made Howie one of the squawkers I had to worry about. It didn't seem fair. Here I was, trying to get rid of my own load of crap, and my old friend hands me even more.

I sighed, looked into my empty glass, and said, "I need another drink." I began to pry myself out of Howie's easy chair. Before I could get to my feet, he said, "Bring the bottle."

I reached the kitchen, wrapped a hand around the jug, and started to turn around. Then I thought — why don't I fetch the ice while I'm at it? I turned back toward the refrigerator, opened the door, and extracted a tray of cubes. I closed the door and started to turn away. I stopped, bemused. The last time I'd been in the room, less than half an hour ago, the refrigerator door had been bare. Now there was a piece of paper scotch-taped to it. A note. I looked. It was addressed to Howie. I called. "Hey, Howie. Someone snuck in here and stuck a note on your fridge."

I heard his chair creak. "Sure." He entered the kitchen as I was setting the ice tray down to keep my fingers from freezing. He looked. "By time, there is. Wonder who?"

"Read it, why don't you."

He did. He peeled it off the door, unfolded it, and slowly spelled it through. I read, too, over his shoulder, aware of his lips moving in the corner of my right eye. The note was short. It said: *Arriving soon, one companion. Let's go fishing. (I told you I'd be back).*

It was signed "Oscar."

I said, "I will forever be damned. I thought sure we'd seen the last of him."

"He said he'd be back."

"He did, at that." I paused, thinking. Then I looked at Howie. I said, "Goose Pond?"

He hesitated for just an instant. Then he grinned wickedly. "Why not?"

When I got home later that night, Bonny was waiting for me. I knew she was there when I saw the light in the living room window. I never left it on when I went out. The electricity was too expensive, and besides, we didn't have to worry about burglars in our town. Not that there weren't any, but they weren't common.

Anyway, I walked in and there she was. I stood there, looking at her and feeling glad that I'd given her a key. She fitted that room the way my ex-wife never had. Dark hair worn short, a tautly swollen figure, intelligent eyes, and a loved and lovable mouth. I liked to look at her. I had ever since I first hired her for my secretary. I would even after I made her something more, I was sure. I was already planning it.

She let me look for maybe half a minute while she finished a paragraph in the book she was reading. Then she closed the book, set it down beside the electric percolator on the table next to her chair, and laid a hand on the pot. Only then did I notice the two cups, the cream and sugar, beside the pot. She said, "I thought you might like some coffee."

And that was Bonny. There I'd been, out drinking. It was late, and we both had work to do in the morning. But if she was annoyed with me, she didn't show it. She was all set to steady my head, to cancel out the booze. She was just what I needed, and I wished she'd been around when I was young. I didn't say so, though. Instead, I accepted a cup and told her where I'd been and what was up.

"You've mentioned that name before," she said. "But not in any detail. Who is Oscar?" She sipped her coffee. She smiled, and I told myself it was time to let the secret go.

"Well, when we met," I said. "When we met, he was fish. A trout." Her eyebrows went up, but she didn't say a thing. I went on. I told her about the marooned saucer pilot, the power shortage that had meant the only locally compatible body his machines could give him was that of a fish, and the contiguity manipulator that let him change the things around him, switching them with their counterparts in parallel worlds to ours. Then I told her about how, when a change was improbable enough, it generated an improbability wave that could be detected by offworld monitors. Finally, I told her how Howie had caught Oscar on a fly tied to imitate a flying saucer.

The coffee was gone before I finished. Her eyebrows had fallen to a more normal position too, and when I was done, all she said was, "And you're taking him fishing?"

"Ayuh," I said.

Then we went to bed.

It was two days later that I came out of a sound sleep wondering what was wrong. I didn't move. I was curled spoon-fashion against Bonny's rump, my nose being tickled by her hair. One arm was folded over her side, the hand cupping her shoulder. We were both sticky with sweat. A gray light was seeping past the curtains. The sun was just barely up.

The phone rang again. I unwrapped myself from Bonny, patted her hip when she murmured a sleepy protest, flipped my side of the sheet out of the way, and padded barefoot out to the kitchen. The phone rang twice more before I reached it. And when I did get it off the hook, it was Howie's voice that assaulted my unready eardrums: "Mornin' Mayor!"

All I could say was, "Do you know what time it is?"

"Ayuh. But Oscar don't."

"Oscar? He's there already?"

"Ayuh. Wants to go fishin', too."

Well, I wasn't going to miss that for anything. "Give me time to grab a bite, then. I'll be over as soon as I can."

I hung up, turned around, and there was Bonny, wrapped in her robe, a billow of half-transparent cloth. Looking at her, I felt more like going back to bed than walking out of the house. She glanced at my feelings and grinned. "Oscar?" I nodded. "You go get dressed, then. I'll put the coffee on."

In twenty minutes, I was as thoroughly ballasted with coffee and donuts as I needed to be. I kissed Bonny goodbye and took off.

It took me five minutes to get over to Howie's place, a trim brick ranch he owed to Oscar's last time around. When I walked into the kitchen, Howie was pouring coffee into a mug. He handed it to me. I sipped. I stared at him for a moment. There was something peculiar about his face, something that might have been a smirk if I hadn't known he was incapable of such an expression. He didn't say a word, but he did nod his head toward the kitchen table.

I turned to look. Two people were sitting there, mugs of their own before them. He was a muscular, slim fellow, Roman-nosed, high-browed, sleek-haired. She was all curves and blonde waves, the stuff of dreams and films. Except for their faded dungarees and checked shirts, they might have been selling expensive liquor in a glossy magazine.

I focused on the man. I said, "Hi, Oscar. Welcome back."

He looked away from me, down at his mug, aside to the woman, with a faint smile on his lips. He seemed embarrassed. If I hadn't been able to see the whiskers on his cheek, I'd have sworn he simpered. He spoke softly, in a high tenor. "Call me William."

"Sure, Bill," said Howie.

Then the woman giggled, and her voice was a marvel. Throaty and warm, the sort of voice that sends shivers up and down a male spine. Including mine. "I'm Oscar," she said.

So I didn't say a word. I couldn't. We'd goofed with that name. And what a goof! Of course, we'd have known better if we'd cleaned her, but then. . . .

"William is my mate this season," she added. She smiled as she said it, implying volumes. Perhaps she thought her rescuers still needed rewards, though she'd done us favors enough already. "But when do we go fishing? I am looking forward to being on the other end of the line."

"Tomorrow, then?"

"Early'd be best. 'Bout dawn."

"All right. That will give us time to be sightseers."

"I'll put you up here for the night."

I wondered what Emma would think of that when she got home.

I was up early the next morning, early enough to be at Howie's by five. It was an ungodly hour, but sometimes a fisherman just has to do it. The fish feed best just after dawn. Twilight comes a poor second; it's more popular with fisherman only because it's easier to be awake then.

Howie had laid on a big breakfast of pancakes and sausage and coffee. We were all eating, stoking up for the long morning ahead, while Oscar told me about the day before.

"It was very funny," she was saying. "He has named the place I used to live the Oscar pool. It looks quite different from this point of view."

"Different time of year, too," I said. "The water's lower now."

"But I was there for a whole year," she said. "I saw it when the water was low, and when the surface was frozen, and when the water ran through like a tachtrain. But always from below. Never from the air."

Tachtrain? For just a moment, I wondered what that was. But then I remembered another incident, one that cost us Keith Hutchison and, for a time, Lydia Seltzer. I would have to ask about Keith before she left, I told myself. But she must have caught the expression on my face, because the next thing she said was, "Oh, yes. I heard about the boy who caught the train here. He is in school now. Perhaps he will learn to be a *spruleer* pilot."

His father would love that. His son, manning a flying saucer. Maybe even with his own contiguity manipulator. I didn't say a word. I just nodded, while William made some remark about how oddly satisfying Howie's simple robust fare was. Nobody responded to him. Food was food, after all, and everyone knew that not all tourists had the manners of an Oscar, the lady who was already tucking into her second stack of cakes.

After a suitable pause, while she swallowed what was in her mouth, Oscar said, "But I am looking forward to the fishing. I want to catch one of those creatures I resembled for awhile." She reached over to lay a hand on William's arm. "They are so sleek and lovely, dear. I know it's hard to believe, but there are times when I actually miss that body."

I almost laughed. No man I knew would trade her for a fish, not even a record-smashing forty-pound brook trout. But I could see her point. A fish had all the advantages in water, and a trout was the perfect design for speed and power and grace. For that he had his fans, fisherman who would never look at another fish, except perhaps salmon.

And then we were done. I lit my pipe. Howie started his morning chew. We left the house and hit the road for Goose Pond. William and I took my car. He didn't say much beyond remarking on the primitiveness of my machine; I wasn't liking him much. Oscar went with Howie in his pickup, hitched to a trailer full of boat and motor. Tucked into the bow of the boat was Howie's immense tackle box, the size of a small suitcase, with his supply of reels and lures and flies. Leaning against the rear seat was a bundle of rods, more than we could possibly need for just the four of us. There must have been a dozen rods, Howie's whole inventory, and among them was one massive anomaly. The butt was as thick through as the tip of a baseball bat. I supposed he used it when he was out in the bay. It was certainly overkill for any fish he could hope to find in fresh water.

Except for the company, the drive was pleasant enough. It was early August and, though the heat of the day was still some hours off, the air was fragrant with new-mown hay. The sky was the clear blue, touched with rose, of early morning.

Clouds were scarce and small. The sounds were of birdsong and cows demanding to be milked, totally unlike the cities I had visited from time to time in my life. I wondered how city-dwellers stood it.

Once at the landing on the pond, it didn't take long to get on the water. Howie backed the trailer until the boat's stern was afloat, winched the boat the rest of the way in, and drove off to park. Then he hooked up the gas line, pressurized the tank, started the motor, and we all boarded. He headed us down the pond toward deep water, throttled back to trolling speed, and said, "There's a bar off the point up ahead. That's where the fish'll be."

There was a light breeze on the pond, just enough to ruffle the water. Perfect fishing conditions. The boat was steady, the heat wouldn't get to us later on, and the fish couldn't see us. We were all set, and it took only a few minutes to get our lines in the water. Fiberglass rods, trolling reels, and streamers. A Nine-Three for Howie, Grey Ghosts for our guests, and a Golden Ghost, a local design, for me.

Within an hour, we all had fish. The smallest, mine, was a three-pound salmon. The largest, William's, weighed all of six and a half pounds. And all of us were happy. Except William. Howie had barely netted his salmon before he was asking, "Is this all we're likely to catch?"

"Ayuh," I said. "There's bigger fish here, but not many. That one's a good size." My line was still in, reeled in, where I'd put it to be out of his way. So was Howie's. But Oscar was already letting hers out again. Her fly was maybe fifty feet behind the boat, just under the surface. We could see the strike, the silvery torpedo rising from below and smashing the streamer, flying into the air. She set the hook, conversation stopped, and the struggle went on. A salmon is a glorious opponent, flashy, leaping, tail-walking, but it tires in time. Hers did, and Howie slipped the net under it as she drew it alongside the boat. She got her hand behind its gills and lifted it free of the netting, worked the hook out of its jaw, and slid it back into the water, just as she had her first. She had been a fish. She sympathized, even though her face was glowing with excitement.

William repeated his complaint. "These are all pretty small." Oscar's latest would have gone four pounds. Not huge, maybe, but hardly small. "Isn't there anything more challenging around here?"

Oscar looked at him. I — anyone — could see that she didn't agree with him. But he was her mate. She said, "The last time we went fishing was on Elros III. The fish aren't fish there, but they are bigger."

"Huh!" said Howie. "We'll see." He took William's rod away from him, removed the streamer, unclamped the reel from its seat, and reeled in the line and leader. Then he said, "Hey, Oscar. Hand me that big rod."

She turned to the sheaf of rods behind her seat. She inspected them to see what he meant, found the baseball bat, and extricated it from its companions. "This one?"

"Ayuh." Howie took it, fitted the reel to its butt, and threaded the line through the guides. He clipped off the nylon leader with his teeth. Then he bent over to rummage in his tackle box. In a moment he emerged with a hook whose likes I had never seen before. It was a foot long and six inches across the bend. "Horse mackerel," he said.

"That's more like," said William. "If there's anything big enough to swallow it."

"There is," I said. A tuna hook. I wondered if Howie had ever used it in fresh water as I watched Oscar watching him fasten a wire leader to the line and the hook to the leader. I nodded when Howie told me, "Your salmon's about the right size, Mayor," and I grinned as Howie threaded that fish on the hook as if it were a smelt.

When he was done, Howie handed the rod to William and said, "Try this." Then he straightened the boat out onto its previous path and we began to troll again.

William looked skeptical. His mouth was tightly pursed, as if he had bitten into a lemon. But he went along with the gag. He lowered his massive bait into the water and let out line until it was dragging a good hundred yards behind us. Then he braced the butt of the heavy rod in his crotch, holding it against the drag of the salmon with both hands. When he was ready, I began to let my own streamer out again. I stopped when Howie touched my knee and shook his head. "He'll need searoom," he said. I nodded and reeled in.

Oscar watched the byplay curiously. She didn't know what we were figuring for her man, but she could see we had something in mind. At the same time, she had confidence in William. She didn't say a word.

We trolled like that for an hour, skeptical, watchful, and patient. Nothing happened. William's bait was too big to interest another salmon — at least I thought so, though I had heard tales — and nothing else showed up. We had gone nearly the length of the pond, and we were almost out of deep water. The bottom shelved upward as we approached the dam at the outlet. But the water didn't really get shallow until after the island ahead of us, and there was one last deep hole first. The island was all rock and pine. I suspected the rock went all the way to the pond's bottom, full of clefts and overhangs, denning places for William's prey.

Howie wasn't about to take us into the shallows. As we neared the island, he began to swing slowly to the left, bringing us into a turn over the hole. This slowed the movement of William's bait, and it settled deeper.

That's when it happened. William's rod tried to bend double, though it was too stiff for that. It bucked, as if he had snagged a sunken log, and I ached in sudden sympathy for his crotch. He should have known better than to brace it there. But he only gasped as he loosed the drag and line ripped off the reel.

Howie was marvelous. He had the boat around and the engine roaring in pursuit in an instant. "Reel in! Reel in!" he cried. "Don't give her slack!" I was speechless. So was Oscar. All we could do was hang on while we careened on a down-east version of a Nantucket sleigh-ride, watch while William fought his would-be catch, gasp when the thing finally leaped almost clear of the water, showing its half-ton body, flippers, the long tail, the longer neck topped by a four-horned head. The jaws were magnificent, full of shark-like teeth that caught the sun and gleamed. Even at our distance, we could see the salmon hanging from the mouth, the hook embedded in the jaw. We broke our silence with a cheer, though I still don't know whether we were cheering for William or the beast.

The fight lasted just over two hours. Nessie was large, but pound for pound she didn't have the stamina of a trout or salmon. She tired quickly, just a little more quickly than William. By the time he had her beside the boat, he was panting, his eyes were beginning to glaze, and his arms were trembling. But he still had strength enough to grasp one scaly horn and lift the massive head from the water. He stared at it, awed, I supposed, relieved, impressed, but too exhausted for triumph. I stared myself. This was the closest I had ever been to a Nessie. A bushel of head. Eyes that met our own with a reptilian implacability. Four horns, right enough, though two of them were more like stubby tentacles. The other two bore the nostrils on their tips. They whistled as the thing fought for breath.

No one moved for at least a minute. We were all suspended in a moment of primitive victory, facing the end of a glorious battle, of a hunt with only simple weapons against a worthy prey. Howie broke the silence when he drew his knife and reached for the line. He spat over the side and said, "This one's pretty small. We only keep the big ones."

William gasped, shocked. He let go the horn to grab Howie's wrist. "But, but. . . . The head!"

Nessie chose that moment to revive. She'd caught her breath. Now her head surged back, her body convulsed, and the line began again to leave the reel. Howie lost his chance to cut the line as William got both hands back on the rod and heaved against the beast's desperate pull. But he wasn't braced as well as he had been. He lost his balance and hit the water.

To Nessie, this had to be more like it. One man offered much less resistance than a boatful. She put on speed, while William kept his grip on the rod. She towed him, faster and faster, while his head cut a brow wave to match the boat's. But it couldn't last. Soon enough, William swallowed too much water. He passed out and let go the rod. Nessie was free, as she deserved to be.

William did survive. Howie had the boat alongside as soon as he stopped moving, and we wasted no time in getting him inboard and over a seat. I worked on him, squeezing the water out of his lungs, breathing for him, while Howie headed back for the landing at top speed. Oscar helped me for awhile, using her contiguity manipulator to trade air for the water in her mate, but as soon as he was able to sit up, coughing and pale, she left him. She moved up front to sit beside Howie. I could see her talking quietly into his ear — shouting, really, above the noise of the engine, but I couldn't hear. All I heard was William, saying how he wished he had a trophy. He'd never had anything like that beast on a line before, and now no one would believe him. He shook his head, sadly, exhaustedly, and said, "I wouldn't have believed it myself."

It wasn't until later, after our guests had gone, that I found out what Oscar had been saying to Howie. It was night again, an hour after the saucer had come to pick them up. Bonny was there, sitting on the arm of my chair, and we all had drinks. Howie was saying, "Cost me a good rod, but it was worth it. Ayuh, it was. Never thought I'd see Nessie so close."

I agreed. Bonny murmured something about, "But wasn't it dangerous?"

Howie said, "'Course. That's the fun of it. 'Sides, way Bill was talkin', he had it comin'."

"Ayuh," I said. "Oscar seemed to think so, too. At least, she didn't spend much time on him once we hauled him in. Talked to you, instead."

Howie grunted and ran his knobby fingers through his hair. It was dirty, as usual, and graying. It had been years since he was young. "Wanted me to come with her, just as soon as Billy's contract was up. Said I'd make a better mate."

I laughed. Bonny asked, "What did you tell her?"

"Told her 'Thanks,' but I'm already married. And Emma wouldn't permit it."

Gambling Man

Howie Wyman had been known to tinker. He had a shop in his barn where his deft fingers, so knobby you wondered how he bent them, could fix a washing machine or a chain saw, build a motorbike or a chest of drawers. Could, I say, and did, too, at times. More often, he just fiddled around with assorted parts, piecing them together, taking them apart, winding up with contraptions that whirled and buzzed and blinked. One of them once earned him a blue ribbon in the Waldo County Regional Arts and Crafts Show. Kinetic sculpture, the judges called it.

But this story isn't about Howie's lone attempt at art. Not that he was trying to make art. He thought he'd built something that would keep the starlings out of his strawberry patch. It worked, too, until Betty Hawkins, our librarian, spotted it and insisted he loan it to her for the show. She was hard to refuse.

This story *is* about something else Howie put together one day. What makes it a story is that Howie's damned tinkering brought the Mafia — the Cosa

Nostra, the Syndicate, the Black Hand, whatever you call it, the folks who run most of the gambling in this country — to our town. It brought a junior godfather, a skinny fellow in tailored brown, elevator shoes, and a shiny Lotus. He had buck teeth and a receding hairline, and he didn't look like a rat. Far from it. For one thing, he didn't have a tail. For another, his nose was too broad. And his ears weren't pointed.

His name was Vincent Conant. Bonny showed him into my town hall office, he took a seat, and when she had closed the door behind her, he said, "Mayor Bowen."

I inclined my head. That was what strangers called me. Friends called me Harry. "What can I do for you?" I asked.

He didn't answer right away. Instead, he reached into the breast pocket of his jacket, extracted a small, cream-colored card, and handed it across my desk. I accepted it. My fingers told me the printing was embossed. I read it. It gave his name and said he was the representative of something called "Counterchance." I must have looked perplexed, for he then said, "I am a consultant. To the gambling industry."

Ah. Now I knew. I carefully refrained from looking at the TV set on the bookshelf to the left of the door. I had wondered how long our luck would last, how long we could keep getting away with it. "And?"

He crossed his legs and plucked at his trousers. He glanced out the room's one window behind me, toward the firehouse across the street, at the color of the trees beyond. He sniffed as if the view didn't suit him. "I have been asked to find an explanation for your extreme good fortune," he said. He paused. "And to stop it."

"Ayuh," I said. I picked up the pipe I had set aside when Bonny knocked. I tamped the ashes down and lit it. I blew a cloud of smoke over Conant's head. "But you can't stop luck. You have to wait for it to turn. It always does."

He stared at me. No, he wasn't a rat. His eyes seemed more reptilian at the moment. "Usually," he agreed. "But for the past six weeks, you have been placing bets on horse races, football games, anything my clients offered odds on. And you have not lost once. It is as if you had access to tomorrow's papers."

I laughed, still not looking at the TV set. "You or your bosses have been smoking the wrong stuff. I'm just lucky."

He didn't buy it. He stood up, set his hands on the edge of my desk, and looked down at me. I had to lean back in my chair to meet his eyes. "You have cost us too much," he said. "You have a system. I want it. I will have it."

I laughed again. I wanted him to think I didn't find him threatening at all. But the laugh was a lie. His threat was real, if implied, and I was suddenly aware of my guts. It wasn't a pleasant feeling. I repeated the only secret I intended anyone besides Howie or Bonny to share. "I'm just lucky."

He stared down at me for another minute. "Sure," he said. He straightened, turned toward the door, turned back, and said, "You will not be able to place any more bets, of course." He turned again and left.

I was glad to see him go, glad to be able to look at the TV set that — had he but known it! — had brought him here. A moment later, Bonny came in, closed the door, and leaned against it. I shifted my gaze to her. My Bonny. My secretary, my fiancee. Intelligent, sympathetic eyes; short, dark hair; an armful of a figure. I had loved to look at her since the day I'd hired her. I still did, all the more because I now knew what her light-blue pants suit concealed.

She broke the silence with, "He sounded like Mafia."

I nodded. What secretary doesn't listen in when she can?

"It's not good, Harry. That bunch'd do anything to get their hands on the thing."

We both looked at the TV set. I agreed, but. . . . "When it comes right down to it," I said, "I'd rather they got it than the government or the insurance companies."

"I suppose." The TV didn't look like anything special. And it wasn't, really. Howie hadn't modified the TV at all. But the antenna leads went to an old hifi amplifier with one tube burned out. The amplifier in turn was hooked to an antenna Howie had concocted. *That* was what was special.

Last April, when the ice had been too soft for ice fishing and the water in the brooks had been too high for the trout to bite, when nobody had had any odd jobs for him, Howie had spent a day in the town library. Emma had had it in for him, as usual, and he had felt that anything was preferable to staying home.

Anyway, he'd been leafing through back issues of *Scientific American* and found an "Amateur Scientist" column that said how to build an electric furnace. He built the thing, and by June he was able to use it to coat young raspberry stems with vaporized aluminum. He got the stems out with acid, wired up the resulting prickly tubes, and built a TV antenna. From a distance, it looked normal; the fuzz of tiny thorns that covered the thing was invisible. But Howie thought that fuzz should let his TV pick up short wavelength radiation as well as microwaves. He plugged the amplifier into the circuit just in case the new signals weren't too strong.

I was there in his shop the day he tried it out. He flipped the switch, we waited a minute, and the screen lit up. But what it showed didn't look like any TV show I'd ever seen. The picture was the same on all channels, and it looked for all the world like the middle of our town, though distorted by a shimmer like a heat haze. There wasn't any sound.

We fiddled with the knobs on the TV and the amplifier until the picture became a mite clearer. At the same time, we discovered we could make the picture move, as if the camera were being carried down the street. We brought the view right up to the town hall, found that we could steer it through the wall, and stopped it when we could see an office calendar. The date was two days away. A clock told us it was just over fifty hours off.

And that was what we had. Not only a camera-less TV, but a time-watcher, a time-spy, as well. Now Bonny took two steps, flicked it on, and played with the knobs to make the picture scan across town. We noticed the cloud of smoke simultaneously. She veered her scan path, tracked it down, and I said, "The Jackson house." Flames were breaking through the roof beside the chimney. "Call Bryant," I said. He was the fire chief. "Ask him to get a chimney-cleaning crew out there today." He would listen. We had made enough such requests lately, both of him and of the town's police. The statistics were down, way down, and I knew we were saving people grief. But I wondered what the effect would be if this were done on a larger scale. That it was worth it here and now, I knew even as I spoke to Bonny. The picture changed, the flames and smoke fading to a shadow.

It hadn't taken us long to figure out what the fuzziness in the picture meant. Perhaps my previous exploits had helped, though Bonny had been the one to make the suggestion, and she'd had only hearsay to go on. The picture was a double — multiple — exposure, showing all the possible futures, shaded according to their probability. Nothing was certain unless the picture was clear, and even then the picture could change between now and then.

Bonny was back at the controls again, the phone call finished. Scanning, scanning, coming back to the town hall and the conference room down the hall from my office. She centered on the long table. its top was bare. So we were taking Conant seriously. I supposed we had to. But it was a shame. For more than six weeks now, we had been covering that table with the sports pages so we could read the headlines in advance. The fine print of the text was virtually invisible to us. Word choice was too arbitrary, too improbable, to give us more than a blur. We had some of the same problem with the headlines, of course, but then we only bet when the news was unmistakably clear.

Bonny turned the TV off and crossed the room toward me. She hitched her fanny up onto the corner of my desk, kicked off one shoe, and rested a foot on my thigh. "I wish Howie had left you out of this one," she said. She looked troubled.

I slid a hand up the leg of her pants suit and stroked her calf. I shrugged. "You know Emma. I don't think he wanted it anywhere she might get her hands on it. She tries to keep him on a short rein as it is."

She wiggled her toes. "I guess it's safe enough here. But shouldn't you tell him about Conant?"

I nodded and picked up my pipe again. "I would if I knew where he was."

I didn't have to worry long about finding Howie. He found me. He showed up in the office the very next day, looking as disreputable as ever in worn boots, dirty overalls, and a checked shirt. His shaggy, graying hair stuck out under the brim of a floppy green felt hat. His cheek bulged with the usual wad of tobacco, and as soon as he entered the room, I toed my metal wastebasket out from under my desk. He spat, making a nasty noise, half clang and half rustle.

Bonny followed him in to listen while I told him about Conant. His reaction only proved I didn't understand him perfectly, for all the years I'd known him. I'd expected him to get mad — in as few words as humanly possible, perhaps — but he only looked disgusted. "So that explains it," he said, and he spat again.

"Explains what?" I asked.

"Burgulars," he said. "Last night. Didn't take anythin', but Emma's madder'n hell."

I could imagine. So could Bonny, from the look on her face. "I told you he was a crook," she said.

I waved a hand. "Of course he is." What else could he be, after all? "But what now? Will he break into my house? Yours, Bonny? Here?"

"All of 'em," said Howie.

"Huh!" Bonny spun on a heel and turned to the TV. She yanked it half off its shelf and reached behind it. She disconnected the leads to the amplifier and then unhooked the amplifier from the antenna, which we had mounted in the town hall attic, amidst the cobwebs, dust, and old files. "He won't find anything here," she said.

Howie nodded. I agreed. It was best to hide the evidence, to make the TV just a TV, the amplifier just a broken-tubed shelf ornament. But still, I regretted it.

"Besides," said Bonny. "We don't really need it anymore. We all have plenty of money now."

Sure.

Howie got out of his chair. "Ayuh," he said. "S'pose we do. I'm goin' birdin'."

I envied him. It was fall, the air was crisp and tangy, the woods and fields were brilliant. And the partridge were out there, ready to burst into flight like a bolt — not of lightning, they weren't that fast; but of thunder, they were that noisy — and fall to shotgun blasts. But I was mayor of our town, unpaid but devoted to the job, the voters all agreed. I had my oil business as well, and that took all the time I could give it, now that the cold weather was coming. I would be lucky to go hunting once that fall. Not Howie, though. He could go when he liked, for as long as he liked. He was limited only by the need he felt to earn just enough money to keep Emma at home. Usually, that meant plowing driveways, painting houses, haying, cutting wood, and the like. But not now. He could go for a year on his share of the betting.

I didn't see Howie again for another week, and nothing remarkable happened while he was gone, unless you count the turkey someone tethered to the church bell clapper. I tended to the affairs of my two offices, undisturbed by Conant or anything relating to him. Bonny kept me company at the town hall and at home. She was almost ready to move in with me. In fact, her own house wasn't much more than a mail drop now.

We had just finished supper and were lingering over our coffee, talking, when Howie showed up at the kitchen door. I hadn't heard him drive in, and when I went to the door I didn't see his pickup in the driveway. Then I looked at him through the screen. I stopped wondering about the truck. He was a mess. He stank. There were saddle bags under his eyes. His face was bruised. His hat was missing. And his shirt was torn.

I let him in. His first words were, "Never did get to go huntin'."

I grabbed him by one elbow as he staggered. "What happened?"

Bonny came up behind me. "Good Lord, Howie!" She caught the other elbow. Together we led him to the table and plunked him down. She went to the sink to wet a dish towel. I reached for the jug in the cupboard over the fridge.

We got the story out of him while he sipped whiskey between swipes of the towel. It seemed he hadn't been a mile out of town on the old county road when two characters in a Landrover ran him off the road, waved guns at him, and hauled him off to an old camp in the woods. He thought it was the Peterson camp.

They had tied him to a bunk frame, standing up. They had beat him with fists and pieces of hose. They had quizzed him: "How do you read the future?" "What's the secret?" "How do you read the future?" over and over again. And they hadn't let him sleep, except for catnaps, for a week.

But it hadn't worked. I could have told them that. Howie wasn't very ambitious, but he was a tough old bird. He never said anything he didn't want to say, and you couldn't change his mind with dynamite. Eventually, they had seen that. A third man had appeared, Conant by the description. He had taken a long look at Howie and said, "Turn him loose." The others obeyed, though they drove deeper into the woods before they threw him into the bushes, still tied.

Howie hadn't stopped to sleep before working his bonds loose and hoofing the ten miles back to town. Now he was ready to drop, as soon as we would let him. I stripped his clothes off — his captors hadn't let him loose for anything — and got him into the tub, scrubbed him down, and tumbled him into my bed. Tough as he was, I expected him to sleep till noon. Bonny and I could bunk on the couch.

When I returned to the kitchen, Bonny was holding Howie's clothes at arm's length. "Should we burn these?"

I shook my head. "We can soak 'em in a bucket outdoors. I'll do it if you'll get the coffee going again."

It was another twenty minutes before we could sit down once more. It took that long to hose the worst of the filth off Howie's clothes and change my own outfit. I'd rubbed a bit too close to my old friend for comfort.

By then the coffee was ready and poured. I topped the cups with a splash of brandy, and we both sighed. I said, "I hadn't thought it would come to this."

"But that's who we're dealing with," said Bonny. "Animals! We can't just stop betting."

I nodded glumly and sipped the coffee.

"We have to do something!"

"Like what?" I felt almost as tired as Howie had looked.

"Convince them there's no secret. That even if there is, it's not worth their trouble."

It would be quite a trick, I thought the next day. How do you call a dog off a hot scent? How do you make precognition look like blind, fool luck? I didn't have any ideas, and neither did Bonny. Neither did Howie, when he finally woke up and got enough eggs and bacon into his belly to talk.

I didn't get into the office till nearly noon. By then, Bonny had put in a good morning's work. Howie was home again, dressed in clean clothes from my closet. And I was still stymied.

Vaguely, I thought a look at the future might help. I hooked up the TV and scanned the town. I saw nothing useful, not even a fire. I couldn't even spot the Landrover. I quit, disgusted, and turned to the work that was always waiting. This time it was the agenda for the city council meeting next week. But I didn't get very far; my mind just wouldn't settle down.

Lunch helped. Barbara Johnson ran the diner, and her pie was enough to improve anyone's mood. When I got back to the office, I tried the TV again. That didn't do me any more good than before, but now it didn't discourage me. The big trouble with Howie's gadget was that you couldn't scan time. You were stuck with a fixed focus, so to speak, fifty hours off. So I kept trying. The agenda could wait.

Eventually, my effort was rewarded. It was about five, and I was checking my house for the umpteenth time, scanning right through it on the way to other parts of town. As the view passed through the living room, I stopped. There I was, with Bonny, being tied up with what looked like bell wire and tossed on the couch. The villains were two greasy-looking characters clad in dirty leisure suits. One was tall, fat, and pimply. The other was short and skinny. Both had long hair and grim mouths, but it was the fat one who leaned over Bonny and gave the wire around her wrists an extra twist. She winced.

I watched as the interrogation proceeded. It wasn't pretty. But my attention wasn't entirely on what was being done to us. Instead, I was looking for shadows, for possible outs. A little twiddling with the knobs brought out the blur. A little more showed up a nice one, surprisingly strong. I followed the new action until I began to laugh. I laughed so hard that Bonny opened the door to see what was wrong.

I pointed at the screen with one hand while wrapping the other around her waist. "The answer," I managed to get out. "Day after tomorrow, the whole crew will pack up and go home."

She stared at the TV. She saw the main view and gasped. "Look at . . ." she exclaimed. "How can they. . . ?"

"The shadow, the shadow," I said.

She studied the screen. Finally, she said, "Ah," and grinned. I let go of her to scan the view. I found the broken door through which they would enter. I found the Landrover, parked under a tree down the road, and there I found another useful shadow.

We left the town hall a few minutes later, after dismantling the apparatus once more. On the way home, we stopped at Howie's. I told him what I was planning. He replied with a laugh and said, "I'll be by 'bout eight. You'll need help cleaning up."

Once home, I left Bonny to get supper together while I raided the garage for cedar shingles and shingle nails. I hammered the nails through the shingles till they looked like so many wool carders, and then I took them and a spade down the road. I found the spot where the Landrover would park.

I laid the shingles on the ground, nails up. I shoveled a little gravel over them so they wouldn't show. And then I went back to the house for supper.

After we'd done the dishes, I cached a wire cutter behind the couch cushion. I hunted up my old .22 target pistol, loaded it, and put it with the cutter. I carefully waxed the front hall floor, laid a braided throw rug in place, and strung a piece of stout monofilament fishing line across the doorway between the hall and the living room. Then I fetched in a cinder block and set it beside the bedroom door. At the last minute, I would set the door ajar and balance the block atop it.

I showed Bonny what I'd done, saying, "Just watch your step if you have to use the hall." She nodded and laughed briefly, making a noise that was more of a snort than anything else. Her mouth was a tight line. She was, I think, remembering what she'd seen Fats doing to her.

I wanted to cheer her up, but I didn't succeed till after we'd had a drink and gone to bed. She'd found out a while back that I've always been partial to redheads. She left her head alone, but she did tint one patch of hair. We both like the effect.

In the morning, when we got to the office, we found signs that someone had been through the place. We knew what they'd been searching for, and we knew they must have been feeling frustrated. After all, they hadn't had much success so far. But they hadn't made a mess. Nothing was broken or missing or strewn on the floor, though everything was just a bit awry.

They hadn't found what they wanted. The TV was still on the shelf, the amplifier beside it. I hooked everything up and scanned the town as carefully as I could. It didn't take long to spot Conant's Lotus parked on Church Street, in the driveway of a large old house that had been converted to apartments a few years ago. The house was kept up well, and it still looked like a sea captain's home, though its new status was betrayed by the parking area that had usurped a sizable chunk of the captain's lawn.

I found the Landrover in the garage, which had once been a stable. That was enough to send me scanning through the house, checking apartments until I found our future assailants. Both wore a good coat of bandage. Fats had a cast covering most of his left leg, and his ribs were taped. Shorty's skull was wrapped in gauze, one arm was in a sling, and one bare foot was supported on a hassock. Conant was daubing what looked like iodine on the sole while Shorty winced repeatedly. A roll of bandage sat on the floor beside the hassock.

I called Bonny in from her desk and let her look. She did, too, and with a grin. "Serves 'em right," she said.

"Think we ought to have a word with Thanhauser?"

She looked puzzled.

"I think he's got the emergency room tomorrow night. It'd be a pity if he did too good a job on them."

She brightened. "I'll call him this afternoon." But though we'd made the decision, the picture on the screen didn't change. It hadn't changed the day before either, but then I hadn't quite decided what to do. But now we had, and Fats didn't suddenly start trying to ease his cast. The tape on his ribs didn't suddenly seem too tight. Shorty's sling didn't grow too short or too long. I guessed Dave wouldn't compromise his ethics even in a good cause. Deserve as they might to suffer, he still felt obligated to do the best he could for them. I shrugged and told Bonny, "Don't bother."

Nothing else happened the rest of that day, that night, or the next day, at least till we got home the next night. I got the agenda taken care of, talked the company into boosting my fuel-oil allocation, and disposed of a dozen lesser matters. It was wonderful how my concentration improved once I didn't have the Conant problem to worry about.

When the time came, we went home as usual. We ate supper, I set the cinder block in place, and we sat down at the kitchen table with our second cups of coffee. We knew how things had to turn out, but we were still nervous. Howie's gadget didn't show more than probabilities, after all, and even if everything came out all right, we still had to go through the preliminaries. They wouldn't be pleasant.

They weren't. The kitchen door crashed off its hinges right on schedule. Fats and Shorty charged in waving guns, hustled us into the living room, wired us up, hands behind us, and tossed us onto the couch. Then they began the interrogation, starting with Bonny. I supposed they wanted to have the fun part first. Then again, maybe they thought I'd break when I saw what Bonny was going through. But I was never further from breaking. The torn clothes, the indignities, the pain, they only made me frantic to get my hands loose and start *my* program.

They didn't even look at me, and they never noticed my gropings behind the cushion as I found the cutter, right where it was supposed to be, cut the wire at the cost of only a little skin, and then found the pistol. They didn't notice a thing until I plugged Shorty right through the biceps of his outstretched arm, and then it was too late.

"Freeze!" I said. If they heard, they didn't show it. Shorty rolled one way, Fats the other. I banged shots in their directions. That kept them from stopping long enough to draw their own guns. Shorty threw himself at the bedroom door, executing a perfect backwards somersault that left his head in position for the cinder block. It smashed his chin into the floor and left him out cold. Fats found his feet and ran for the front hall. He tripped over the fishline, landed on the rug, and cartwheeled into the wall with an audible crack of bone. He was out too.

Bonny was laughing, but there were tears in her eyes as well. Hysterics. I told myself that was no surprise as I cut her loose. Things had happened awfully fast. We'd gone from down to up in thirty seconds, and even though we'd known what would happen, it had to have an effect.

I let her go on while I collected the bad guys' guns and raided their wallets for their papers and cash. There was quite a lot of the latter. I guessed it was their pay for the job. I figured we had a better right to it, and, besides, it didn't seem a bad idea to add insult to injury.

By then, Bonny had calmed herself down. I tossed my take on the couch beside her and said, "We can replace that dress."

She grimaced — that didn't matter — and said, "What are you going to do with them now?"

"Nothing. Throw 'em out." I shrugged. "What else?"

"I wish I had a sharp knife."

"That'd be gelding the lily, wouldn't it?"

"Try me." She stretched her arms and stood up. She walked over to Shorty and kicked him in the ribs, none too gently. He opened his eyes and glared up at her. "So throw 'em out. I'll get a mop. For the blood."

I did what she said. I grabbed Shorty by the collar and hauled him past his buddy, out the front door, and onto the lawn. I slapped Fats in the face until he came around, and then I hauled him out too. They struggled to their feet, Fats' broken leg dragging, and I told them, "Tell your boss from me that we were lucky. Maybe he'll believe me now."

And that was it. As soon as they were out of sight, I went back inside; Bonny and I had a brief spell of the shakes — what if the probabilities hadn't worked out? — and Howie showed up with the shingles, a toothy grin, and the laconic report, "Three flats. And the little one stepped on a shingle." Bonny changed, and we cleaned up the blood and bits of wire and crumbs of cinder block, and put the fishline back where it belonged. Then I poured the booze and we all sat down.

Howie wanted to take his antenna apart and forget it had ever existed. I agreed. "If we keep it," I said, "it's only a matter of time before someone else gets wind of it. We might not be so lucky next time."

"Could do a lotta good, though," said Howie as he topped off his glass.

"I don't know," said Bonny. "You got it out of the house awfully quick."

Howie shrugged. I said, "That was Emma."

Bonny looked at me across the table. I wasn't sure just what her expression meant. "Well," she said. "Isure don't want it around this house once were're married."

"Ayuh." I was suddenly uncomfortable. "It wouldn't do much for trust, would it?"

"I know one thing. It would take all the surprise out of Christmas."

Roll Them Bones

I finally gave Bonny the ring the week before Christmas. I did it over drinks at the Foxfire, the new restaurant in Dick Witham's Oak Lane Shopping Center.

Bonny wasn't surprised. After all, we had been living together, more or less engaged, for over a year by then. She knew me, and she had to know the time was ripe. Still, she raised her eyebrows when I fished the gift-wrapped package from my jacket pocket, said, "Oh, Harry!" when she'd opened it, and leaned across the table to kiss me.

Ignoring the smiles of the other diners, I took the ring and fitted it onto her finger. She held it up to admire it. The stone wasn't big — maybe a quarter carat — but it caught the candlelight and sparkled just the way a diamond should.

I sipped my scotch and said, "Want to set a date?"

Her drink was a manhattan. She didn't touch it as she answered. "I've always thought New Year's Day would be nice. Is it possible?"

"We'll have to see."

Our table was near the Foxfire's big picture window. We had a good view of the slope twenty feet below, of the trees silhouetted against the snowy ground, of the stream beyond, rocks crusted with frozen spray. The glass gleamed with reflections of the candles on the restaurant's tables, dim images of diners and their silverware. I glanced at Bonny in the glass, the soft green of her dress, the curves of neck and arm and bust. I had loved to watch her since the day I hired her, a secretary for a small-town Mayor. I thought I always would, even if, like now, I couldn't always meet her eyes. Her attention was for the room's interior.

She spoke softly. "This is an eerie place, Harry."

I followed her gaze. "I suppose it is." The walls glowed with phosphorescent skeletons and skulls and gravestones. Bats were painted on the ceiling. The tablecloths were black. The waiters and waitresses wore loose tunics meant to suggest shrouds. I pointed with a breadstick. "Those stones would have been real, not plaster, if it hadn't been for Howie. Or this place wouldn't have been built. Take your pick."

This time she sipped her drink and I left mine alone. "I heard about that," she said. "The strike and all. But I was away that month. I didn't get back till it was all over."

True, I thought. I had forgotten for a moment. Though I shouldn't have. God knows I had missed her enough while she was settling her mother's estate.

"But I didn't hear Howie was mixed up in it. Tell me."

"Let's order first."

The story had really begun just over a year ago, when Dick Witham had looked me up in the office of my oil business. I was at my desk, working over the piles of paper, bills to pay, bills to send out. It was a one-man operation, except for the drivers, but that was enough for our town, with its 6,000 souls.

Dick hadn't made an appointment, but that didn't matter. If I'd been with someone else, he'd have waited or come back later. As it was, he waltzed in, unzipped his jacket, pulled the other office chair up to the corner of my desk, and said, "Hi, Harry."

Dick was a little less than average height, fortyish, and thick-bodied. His thinning hair was brushed straight back, and the rims of his glasses were almost invisible. He looked more like a desk-bound clerk than a successful realtor and insurance agent.

I took a second to finish adding up a column of figures on the calculator, wrote the answer down, and used a burner nozzle for a paperweight. "Hello yourself," I said. I gestured at my desktop. "Autumn leaves, I call 'em. They blow in here every year about this time. Haven't seen you for a few days, Dick. What's up?"

He waved a hand and grinned without showing his teeth. "Up to Boston," he said by way of explanation. "Bankers, lawyers, architects."

"The shopping center?" I knew he was working on one, collecting permits, buying land, lining up occupants.

"Yup." His voice softened, became a shade huskier. It seemed to emphasize the cologne he wore. "We're almost ready to break ground now. But we do need one more bit of land."

Ah, I thought. If he had wanted to see me as Mayor, he'd have gone to the Town Hall. But he was here. And I did own a few acres around and about.

"The old Cross property. You willing to sell?"

I shrugged. "If the price is right."

"It is. Enough to cover what your father paid for it, plus inflation, plus a profit."

It sounded good. It sounded even better when he named the price he had in mind. Enough cash to make even a profiteer happy. Perhaps, I told myself, there were advantages to dealing with old friends. But though I was willing to sell, I wasn't sure he would really want this particular piece of land when he knew more about it. I said as much, and he laughed. "It's just what we need," he assured me. "Gives us a parcel that just fits the architect's ideas. Good spot for the restaurant, too."

"But there's an old cemetery there, Dick. And an odd story, too."

He looked skeptical. I suggested we have a look at the property before we did anything else.

Twenty minutes later, we were driving down the rutted dirt lane that lead past the graveyard. We came to a sign that read, "Posted Bridge — Limit 5 Tons." We stopped beside the mossy pillars that marked what had once been the cemetery's entrance. The picket fence and gate had long since rotted into the soil, one with the guests it had protected from intrusion. What path there was, overgrown with brambles and low shrubs, flanked by heavy-trunked trees, had been trodden out by deer and hunters, fishermen and berry-pickers. This burying ground had been left to nature more than a century before. I told Dick, "I poked around in here once. Latest stone I found was marked eighteen twenty-three."

He didn't bother to hush his voice. The atmosphere, despite all the bare branches, blowing leaves, and ancient stones, didn't really seem to call for it. The dead were too long gone. "What was the oldest?" he asked.

"Hiram Cross's. That's the one I want to show you."

We left the path to push our way among the oaks and maples and occasional wild cherries. We scuffed leaves, picked an apple, and bore to the left, down the slope toward the stream. We passed graves, few of them with upright stones. They had been heaved by years of roots and frost. Many were flat and broken, their inscriptions unreadable. A few leaned like drunks clutching for nonexistent lamp posts. There were none of the elaborate monuments of less rural cemeteries, no obelisks or mausoleums. All the stones were simple slate or limestone slabs, headstones the size of chairbacks, footstones more like loaves of petrified bread.

We paused where one of the stones had tumbled into the path. It had broken into three pieces, and the breaks were as encrusted with lichen as the original surfaces. We could make out the blurred outline of a cross on one of them. "It has been awhile, hasn't it?" said Dick. He kicked at the ground. "Hah!" I looked. There was a yellow gleam in the forest mould, and in a moment he held a gold ring.

"Better put it back."

He shook his head and slipped the ring onto a finger. "A luck piece. An antique, too."

The sound of the breeze rattling among the boughs and the chuckling of the stream down the hill reminded me, at least, that the dead, deprived of the respect they deserved, could be vengeful. But I said nothing, and in a moment we were at our goal.

Hiram Cross's marker was the largest we had seen, and it was nearly upright, thanks to a trunk that had stopped its lean. The name upon it was clear. The dates below were barely legible.

Dick looked at it for a moment before he spoke. Then he said, "Did you know there's Crosses in my family? My grandmother was one."

I hadn't known. I didn't know what difference it might make, either. I said, "Sixteen sixty-six to seventeen fifty. And an epitaph."

"Ayuh," said Dick. "But you can't read it."

"Not now, maybe." You could count the lines — six — but you couldn't quite make out the words. A letter here and there was clear. The rest was obliterated by lichen and decay. "But you could when I was a kid. At least, you could puzzle it out."

"You remember how it went?"

"I think so." I had been searching my memory ever since he had asked about the property. I could have given him the gist of it without any trouble. But I wanted to give him the whole of it, and he wanted the same thing. After a suitably dramatic pause, I recited:

"For all his days
He grew no moss
At last at rest
His bones ne'er toss
Who stirs his dust
Will count his loss."

Dick laughed. "A traveller, then. And happy to be home at last."

"You don't find it ominous?"

"Not hardly. I'm not superstitious. But what's the story you mentioned?"

We found a log from which we could see old Hiram's stone and sat down. I stuffed and lit my pipe. Dick lit a cigarette. "It was before my time, you understand. Back in the twenties, I believe. Some archeologist down from Boston started digging here. Opened the coffins, collected what trinkets he could, took out the skulls to measure them."

"So?"

I pointed down the hill toward the stream with my pipe. "The day he got to Hiram, that night his car ran off the bridge there. Nearly drowned."

"But what could Hiram have had to do with it?"

I shrugged. "Who knows? But they did find a tooth caught in the steering mechanism, I hear. They put it back in Hiram's jaw, put the skull back in the box, and filled the hole in again. The archeologist went home to Boston."

Dick was silent for a moment. Then he stood up, turned his back on the stone, and said, "It had to be coincidence. A freak accident. Besides, I've lived here most of my life, and I never heard such a thing. You've gotta be making it up."

"Not a bit of it."

"But if you don't want to sell. . . ."

I gestured him back onto the log. "That's not it, Dick, and you know it. I just want you to know what you're up against. Informed consent, they call it."

"Hah!" He must have thought me as hagridden as any Appalachian hillbilly. He should have known better. I had laughed at such things myself, once, but since then I'd learned enough to make me keep an open mind. I'd even learned some of it in the course of my public duties, and he should have remembered that. It would have saved him trouble.

We closed the deal the next week, and that gave Dick all the land he needed for his shopping center. Over the winter, he had a crew in to clear the site, sell off the wood, and burn the slash. Come April, once the mud had firmed up a bit, he brought in another crew to start preparing the construction site. It was about then that we got the phone call about Bonny's mother and she had to leave me for awhile.

Dick brought in three bulldozers, but before they got to the graveyard, he had the stones gathered up and set aside. He was already thinking of how he might use them in the restaurant.

When they did get to the graveyard, all went well at first. All might have stayed well, too, if the ground hadn't been so full of stumps and roots and, as usual in this state of Maine, rocks. But to smooth the ground at all, the dozers had to bite deep. They had to break into the graves and scatter bones and bits of rotten coffins throughout the site.

That was when it happened. All three dozers broke down, and within an hour of each other at that. "How" was no problem — one had a clot of grave mould jammed in its air intake; another had a corroded brass coffin nail through its radiator; the third had a thigh bone caught between the drive wheel and the tread. Nothing disastrous, nothing irreparable, but annoying, time-consuming, and ominous. The "why" was the mystery.

It took the rest of that day and half the next to get the machines fixed and back to work. But it didn't last, and this time the delay was worse. A worker, idle on his lunchhour, was scraping lichen off the stacked gravestones when he discovered Hiram's and read the epitaph. He told his mates, and they unanimously refused to go back to work "till the curse was off."

I heard about the strike when Dick dropped into my office, the one in the Town Hall. With Bonny gone, there wasn't any secretary to show him in, so the first I knew he was there was when he cleared his throat and said, "Mayor Bowen."

I looked up from the grant application I was examining. He was disheveled, his hands were dirty, his suit smudged. "Hello, Dick," I said. "What's up?"

He told me. The breakdowns. The strike. That impossible curse! He still didn't believe in it, but what was he to do?

"It sounds," I suggested, "like you've at least got to go through the motions of taking the hex off. If you want to get the job done, that is." My pipe was lying beside the ashtray. I picked it up, tapped the ashes down, and lit it. I blew a cloud of smoke at the desktop. It fanned out like dust behind an unloading dump truck.

He thought about it. He realized I wasn't telling him the curse was real, and he accepted that. Going through motions was something he knew how to do.

He nodded. He said, "But what do I do?"

"For openers, we go look for Howie Wyman."

Howie was an old friend of mine, an unambitious, odd-jobbing country boy who liked nothing better than fishing and hunting. He usually wore a green felt hat whose brim flapped in the breeze, dirty overalls, faded checked shirts, and well-aged leather boots. Today was no exception, except that the hat was off — his wife, Emma, saw to that when he was in the house — and his shaggy grey head was open for inspection. Not that anyone would want to get too close.

We found him at home, a brick ranch full of aging furnishings Emma kept spotless and shining. She showed us into the living room, where Howie was watching a soap opera, his feet up on a hassock and a beer in his hand. She turned the sound down on the TV, and we all found seats. Dick took the couch, Emma a straight-backed chair. I chose a platform rocker that might have been new when my father was a boy.

When we'd finished saying hello, I said, "Dick's got a problem, Howie. Maybe you can help."

"Ayuh." He drained his beer and fished a plug of linty tobacco from his hip pocket. As he tore a chunk free, Emma got up, crossed the room, and pulled an empty lard can from behind the couch. Her lips were pursed as she set it down beside her husband's chair. She set it down hard.

Dick began to explain the background, but he was hardly through with his description of the project when Emma interrupted. "We @$don't@% need another shopping center," she said. "Downtown should be good enough without taking some poor farmer's fields and. . . ."

We heard her out, and when she ran down, Howie said, "Want to go outside? There's a bench or two by the orchard."

We went, leaving the soap opera to Emma, and Dick picked up his story again. When he was done, Howie spat a dark brown stream toward one of his apple trees. I looked at the tree. Its bark bore a large stain, the mark of Howie's constant target practice, but the tobacco juice didn't seem to have hurt it. It was covered with the tiny green nubbins that, every year, replace the blossoms. I thought of how they would swell, turn red, and touch the air with wine, and my mouth watered.

Howie said, "You're a Cross yourself, ain't you?" Dick nodded and looked interested. Howie added, "Well, old Hiram was a family man, even if he weren't home much. Might count for somethin'."

"What do you mean?" asked Dick. I could see he wasn't too happy. Howie seemed to be taking the curse seriously.

"Can't undo anythin'. But you might mollify him. Put him back to bed and build you a house right over him."

"You mean, give him a family life again?" I put in.

"Ayuh."

"It is a good spot for a house," I added. "The brook and all."

"Impossible!" said Dick. "That's going to be the restaurant. It's in the blueprints." Going through the motions was clearly one thing, but this! This just wouldn't do! Live with a graveyard in the basement? No way! Watching the feelings fly across his face, I almost laughed.

Howie just shrugged. He spat again. "Ayuh. Won't help, but you might replant him in another graveyard."

"@$That@% I'll try," said Dick.

And he did. He talked the workers into gathering up all the bones they could find, tossing them helter-skelter into packing cases, and moving them across town to another old cemetery. He hired a minister to say a few words. Then he covered the old bones up and tried to forget them.

I was on hand for the brief ceremony. So was Howie, and it was clear that my friend did not find Dick's optimism very realistic. When Dick left to get work going again on his shopping center, Howie shook his head and muttered, "Won't work." I don't think anyone heard him but me.

For the next few days, Dick seemed more right than Howie. All went well. The dozers finished preparing the site. The workers knocked forms together and began to pour the footings and walls. But when they got to pouring the walls for the restaurant, walls that would enclose what had been the graveyard. . . .

Dick burst into my office, dressed in overalls and speckled with bits of dry, grey concrete. His eyes were wide and his face was ambiguously blotched, simultaneously flushed and pale. His hands shook. At first, I thought he was angry. Then I said to myself, "He's scared."

He was both. That was quickly clear, as he stumbled into a chair and gasped, "I was right there. And it happened. Just like that. What'll I tell his mother?"

I calmed him down with a drink from the office bottle. Then I got the story out of him. He had been supervising the pouring of the concrete, helping out as necessary. "I was standing right on top of the form," he told me. "And it gave way. I grabbed the mixer's chute, but Sam. . . ." Sam was one of the younger workers on the crew. He had been standing on the ground when the still-liquid concrete burst its restraints, knocked him down, and covered him. Before they could get him out, he had suffocated.

"There was no warning. It didn't creak or groan or anything," said Dick. He held out his glass. I filled it again. And then he gave me the punch line: When they had cleaned up the mess, they had found a jawbone, still caught on the edge of a form plate. The men swore it hadn't been there when they put the forms together, and now they were on strike again.

Somehow, I wasn't surprised. I called Howie, gave him the tale, and he wasn't either. He did, however, say he wanted to see what had happened. Would we meet him there?

There wasn't a worker in sight when we arrived. There was just Howie, pacing the tops of what walls were standing, surveying the layout. We headed across the piles of dirt and rubble toward him. As we passed the construction company's office trailer, the door opened and a small man came out. Dick stopped to wait for him, saying, "That's the architect. Saul Nemmers."

I studied the approaching figure. Nemmers was clad in suntans, with black curls escaping from beneath a visored cap. His face was square, and he wore a toothbrush mustache under a blunt nose. He was younger than I might have expected, still in his twenties.

He didn't say a word when he joined us. He just fell in as we started walking again. When we reached Howie, my friend was staring at the site of the graveyard. He turned to look down at Dick from his vantage atop the wall. "Happened here?"

"You can see the gap in the forms."

"Ayuh." Howie shook his head. He spat into the dust and jumped off the wall to land beside us. "So I was right the first time."

Only then did Nemmers say anything. "What do you mean?"

I explained. Howie thought old Hiram might forgive the shaking up Dick had given his bones if only Dick, a descendant, would give him a family life again. Put Hiram back where he belonged, build a house over his grave, and live in it.

Nemmers opened his mouth. He shut it. He looked thoughtful. Finally he said, "Would an apartment do?"

We all looked at him. I laughed, but wasn't that what architects were for? To solve the problems that plagued any construction project?

Howie must have guessed my thought, for he smiled as he said, "Might."

Dick said, "But the restaurant!"

Nemmers said, "Put it on a second floor. You'd get a better view that way anyway."

And that's the way it worked out. The very next day, while Nemmers revised his blueprints, Dick had the crates full of bones retrieved. Howie solved the problem of sorting Hiram's remains from all the rest by spilling all the bones out in a line, bending two brass rods into L shapes, and walking down the line holding the short legs of the L's in his fists. When the long legs dipped, he had another piece of Hiram.

When Howie was done with his dowsing, Hiram got a new coffin. His neighbors were simply parcelled out into as many piles as there were headstones, one skull to a pile, and packed into cardboard boxes for their third burial. I was sure we made some odd bedfellows that way, but I didn't think they were in any state to mind. Then we laid the stones flat, about where they'd been in the first place, and poured a slab of concrete over the whole shebang. That would be the apartment floor.

Howie spoke to the workers, too, and they came back. Most of them, anyway. There were a few who had been scared enough to look for other jobs. Those who did come back had no more problems. The rest of the work went without a hitch, and the revised design, leaning toward the stream the way it does, was even better than the original. It actually won Nemmers an award.

By the time I'd finished, Bonny and I were both full of white wine and scallops. We were on the cheesecake and coffee, and she was shaking her head. Her lips were pursed as if in disgust, though there was a twitch to the corner of her mouth. "That story doesn't help the atmosphere at all," she said. "Imagine! Eating dinner over a graveyard!"

I nodded and sipped my coffee. "It's a busy place, though. That story doesn't keep folks away."

At that moment, I felt a hand on my shoulder. "Everything all right, Bonny? Harry?"

We both looked up. It was Dick. The owner, circulating among his guests, greeting friends and regulars. His hand, which still wore the gold ring he had kicked out of the dirt, held a glass half full of clear liquid. "Just fine," I said. "Couldn't be better."

"Where did you find your chef?" asked Bonny.

"Dug him up in Portland. I have nightmares they'll want him back." He patted my shoulder, nodded to Bonny, and left to visit another table.

Bonny and I looked at each other. The bags under Dick's eyes were the size and color of used teabags, and his breath smelled of gin. She shook her head, her dark hair bouncing, and said, "I don't think he sleeps enough to have nightmares."

I followed Dick with my eyes. He wasn't married, and bachelors didn't have much of a family life to offer anyone, much less a ghost. I nodded, once. "Hiram was a mite active, you know. Maybe he still is."

Energy Crisis

Jason Wilkins' kidnapping turned our town upside down. It upset the even tenor of our ways, changed our economy forever after, and gave us a taste of international intrigue. Fortunately for our self-respect, it was a local boy who cracked the case, and Howie Wyman at that.

Jason was the six year old son of Abby Gerder and Saul Wilkins. His parents had left Philadelphia to found the Maine Hydroelectric Development Corporation. They had come to town two years ago, bought up the burned-out leatherboard mill at the Bottle Pond outlet, and restored the old dam there. As soon as they could get a generator hooked up, they had begun selling electricity to the power company.

Nobody thought the kidnapping was for money. Abby and Saul didn't have any to speak of. They had sold their house, pawned their possessions, and borrowed every cent they could to get their pet off the ground. And it would be years before they could hope to be solvent again. The Bottle Pond dam produced only a hundred and fifty kilowatts at its peak, just enough to buy groceries. The future depended on all the other dams they intended to restore and put on line. There were more than fourteen hundred abandoned dams in Maine, they would tell anyone who would listen, and a third of them could be restored economically. They had options on a dozen.

And their son was gone. Most folks figured the kidnapper had to be someone who lived on the pond. Feelings were running high, what with the pond's level dropping through that first summer, the summer homes being left with mudflats for lawns, and no prospect of change unless Maine Hydro would stop using its water rights. There had been vandalism, a poisoned dog, letters to the editor, and now this.

I had my doubts, myself. I couldn't believe the people I presided over as Mayor would stoop to such tactics. But I had been wrong before.

At any rate, their son was gone. He had been playing in the back yard of their rented house one afternoon two weeks back. His mother had been at the office by the dam. His father had been inside, looking out a window from time to time to check on the boy. He had missed Jason at once, but there had been no sign. There had not even been a ransom note.

I couldn't remember that we'd ever had a kidnapping in our town before. Still, the town cops knew enough to holler for the State Police and the FBI. Within a day, we were swamped by experts, plainclothes men with shoulder holsters and grim faces, men with experience and an eye for clues. But also men with no luck at all. Jason stayed missing. The reason for the crime remained unknown. There was still no ransom note, though Abby and Saul would have cut their throats to get Jason back. There was not even a body.

Of course, the story actually began the day I agreed to deliver the court order. That was most of a year ago, last summer, when the lake-dwellers had taken their complaints of mudflats and high-handed power companies to a judge. And for all the shortages, the judge had been sympathetic.

I wasn't too fond of the chore, but the sheriff was marrying off his daughter that day, and it did have to be done. I let him palm the papers off on me, and I took a minute to look them over before prying myself out of my swivel chair and asking Howie if he wanted to come along. He'd been trying to persuade me that trout fishing was more appealing than playing Mayor or cutting wood.

As we pulled out of the town hall lot, he said, "Gerder's a fine name for an engineer." I took my eyes off the road long enough to glance at him. As usual, he wore dirty overalls, a checked shirt, and a battered felt hat. Our town's noblest loafer, given to fishing and hunting whenever he didn't feel obliged to find a little cash in odd jobs; he was a friend of mine.

"I suppose so," I grunted as he spat a stream of tobacco juice through his open window. "But what difference will it make?" I liked the woman, and I didn't like what I was about to do to her. I thought the sheriff must feel the same way.

"Not a mite," he said He chewed his cud for a minute. "Had a dentist here once. When you were off to college. Named Slaughter. Annie Blood was his nurse. Didn't stay long."

"I'm not surprised." I'd heard of Slaughter and Blood before. He'd been a good dentist, and Annie was still around, working for a pediatrician. Folks just hadn't liked the combination of names. If he'd stayed, they'd both have starved.

The drive to Bottle Pond didn't take long. The dam at the outlet was already in sight, past the firs and poplars along the river. Twelve feet high and thirty wide, it channeled the water into a silver-painted penstock that followed the riverbed to a concrete powerhouse near the ruins of the old mill. A cleared area separated the ruins from the farmhouse that served Gerder and her husband as an office. The shingles on the walls were stained red. There was a Maine Hydro sign over the door.

We parked next to the office and got out. Saul opened the door for us. A tall fellow, built heavily, he resembled a lumberjack gone to seed. His cheeks looked stubbled despite the patch of tissue on one jaw that proclaimed a recent shave.

His brows flared like misplaced horns. His nostrils were wide enough to pick with his thumb.

He stepped aside as we climbed the steps. "Come on in, Harry. Good to see you again."

"You won't think so in a minute," I said. I wanted to smile back at him, but I couldn't manage it. Saul had worked for the same oil company as his wife, in advertising, I thought. He had staked just as much as she on the move, and here I was with the stopper. I didn't like the way I felt. "Abby in?" I added.

He hooked a thumb over his shoulder. "Inside." We entered. The room was large, its antique paneling dark with layers of varnish. Long tables in the middle of the floor were covered with blueprints, documents, sketches, and sheaves of notes. Bookshelves sagged along the walls. In one corner, a new metal desk flanked a photocopier. The opposite corner held an old rolltop, and there was Abby. Where her husband was heavy, she was drawn wire-thin. Nearly as tall as he, she was all planes and angles, nerves and energy. Her greying hair only made the resemblance to a greyhound stronger.

She swiveled her chair toward us. "What's this?" she said. "What do you mean, Harry, we don't want to see you? Is it that injunction?"

I nodded. I pulled the envelope from my jacket pocket and held it out to her. I said, "You're to keep the lake level between one and two feet from the top of the dam."

"Ha," she snorted. "It won't be that high again till fall. It's down three already, and it looks like a dry summer." And hollering wouldn't do the lake-dwellers a bit of good, I knew. Even a judge can't make it rain.

Abby got out of her chair and crossed to a big knife-switch on one wall. She pulled it down. "That turns it off," she said. "We won't make things any worse. But don't you think it stops us!"

"Ayuh," said Howie. "Things get bad enough, 'n they'll be beggin' you to give 'em lights."

"That's not what I mean," she said. She grinned. "It's just that we barely need the lake." She pointed back at her desk, at a small object resting on its peak. I picked it up. It looked like a brass model of the penstock and powerhouse outside, but there was a curious twist to it. The penstock portion ended in a large funnel, a flashlight bulb was screwed into the roof of the generator building, and an electric cord trailed away from the side. Odd as the additions were, though, the twist was something else. My eyes were having trouble following the merger of penstock and powerhouse.

"I'll show you," she said. I handed it to her. She pushed papers aside on a table, set it down, and plugged in the cord. My eyes widened when the bulb failed to light but the whole device took on a liquid sheen and the twist grew worse. "It's based on a Klein bottle," she told us. "Two Mobius strips glued edge to edge. You can't really build one in three dimensions, but with a little power and some electronics, you can get at the fourth dimension."

Saul brought her a cup of water. She poured it into the funnel. There was a whir, as of a tiny generator, the bulb glowed, and I could have sworn water was flowing over the outside of her device. It kept on for a good five minutes before the water began to run out where a tailrace should have been. She caught it in the cup.

"The inside of a Klein bottle is the same as the outside," she said. "So this thing recycles the water. Scale it up and put it in the shack out there, and we could run forever. We'd hardly touch the lake level."

"Gonna do it?" asked Howie.

"Of course," said Abby. "We've already filed for the patents, and Delco is working on the big one now. We'll install it next month."

I hoped it would work. I liked Abby and Saul. I knew we needed the power, and I thought the people who believed a dam's sole function was to give them high water for their boats and beaches were a bunch of fatheads. And Abby might have found the perfect technological fix. But as we drove away, Howie Wyman spat out his cud and said, "I don't like it, Mayor. Somethin' for nothin' just ain't right."

I trusted Howie's thoughts. He had been right too often in the past for me to doubt, and now he had me less than certain.

We certainly weren't used to getting something for nothing. Nothing for something was more like it, or worse than nothing. We put time, money, and effort into building a civilization, we invest in "progress," and what do we get? Shoddy goods, foul air, fouler water, and noise. We thought we could have utopia, peace and quiet and plenty for all.

Well, perhaps that could come yet. The machines were faltering already, there were fewer cars on the road every year, and oil was scarce enough to put a real crimp in my business. I was being forced to shift over to firewood, stockpiling the logs, hiring school kids to cut and split, delivering. At a bill and a half a cord, it was worth my while and there was enough profit for all concerned. Even for Howie, who played foreman for me from time to time.

For the next few weeks, I tended to what was left of my oil business. I spent more time ripping out the old oil furnaces and installing woodburners. I even got in some time at my town hall desk, tending to the town's business. I would have got in more if being Mayor paid at all, but the job was an elective honor, a tribute to my luck in solving unusual problems. Someday I'll tell the truth about Howie and let him have the job.

That someday seemed a lot closer now. When Bonny and I got married last New Year's, she decided she shouldn't be my secretary anymore. I saw her point, though I balked at letting her quit. My wife was a fetching dark-haired bundle of competence. I had liked to look at her since the day I'd hired her, and she never made me regret it.

But she did quit. She insisted, and I had to find another, half as attractive and a tenth as competent. Louise was attractive enough, though she lacked the intelligence and ready empathy that shone in Bonny's face. She had gone to secretarial school, too, and she had a few years of experience, but she was prone to scheduling three appointments for the same time. I was giving her hell for that when the phone rang.

I said, "I'll get it," and waved her out of the office. She left with a "Why does everybody blame me?" petulance on her face. As soon as the door closed, I grabbed the receiver. It was Bonny. I told her I wished she'd come back to work. "Your sub is driving me mad."

The telephone company turned her laugh into a tinny buzz. "Then you shouldn't have married me."

"The hell I shouldn't." I was relaxing already. She had that effect on me. "But what's up?"

"Have you seen the paper? Page six?"

"Not yet. What is it?"

"Take a look. You'll see."

We chatted for a moment more before we hung up. Then I opened my door and told Louise to bring me the paper she'd had her nose in when I'd arrived earlier. She did, not looking at me, and I found the article. It was on Maine Hydro. Abby's new power plant was working, and its efficiency, according to the reporter, was phenomenal. It was producing a healthy 300 kilowatts now, when the flow it could use was drastically restricted. The reporter didn't understand how it worked, but he was sure Abby had just revolutionized the whole concept of hydro power.

I wasn't sure he was wrong. Efficiencies on the order of a thousand percent were certainly revolutionary. But could they be real? I decided it was time for another visit to the dam, the more so because I didn't want to watch Louise hash anything else up. She would, too. I would bet on it.

Maine Hydro's parking lot was full of cars. Reporters, I thought, until I spotted a couple of sidedoor insignia. Bureaucrats. At least one all the way from Washington. I got out of the car and looked toward the powerhouse. It had the same wet sheen, the same unseeable twist, as the model. I could hear the machinery whirring, smell a trace of ozone. She had it working, all right.

No one held the door for me this time. I let myself in and stared. The room was crowded. There must have been two dozen people there. I spotted Saul, Abby beside him, bent over a blueprint flattened on a table. Someone was saying, "It reminds me of an Escher print."

"Exactly," said Abby. "That's really what gave me the idea. Though of course I couldn't build it the way he drew it. That's impossible."

No one laughed. Instead they listened intently as she explained how she tapped the fourth dimension to make her Klein bottle possible and powered the tap with the generator's own output. She sounded like she had already explained it all many times today, but she never flagged. She pointed to a row of indicator dials and rheostat knobs on the wall. "That dial shows the flow in the penstock," she said. "That one shows the power output. That knob lets us control the bore in the 4D part of the bottle. It lets us vary the recycle efficiency."

"How's it work?"

Saul stepped to the wall and twisted the knob. Abby said, "By increasing the bore, we can increase the output without increasing the water flow. Actually, within limits, we can get more output with less flow."

Everyone in the room was quiet as they watched the output needle move across its dial. The other dial really did show a reduction in the flow through the penstock Saul allowed just time enough for the demonstration to sink in. Then he turned the knob back to where it had been before. Abby said, "Of course, we're limited by the capacity of the generator. If we up the output too much, we'll burn out the coils."

Beautiful, I thought, as I edged through the mob toward Abby. When I reached her, I tapped her on the shoulder. She looked at me and grinned. I said, "Looks like the folks at the lake don't have to worry now."

She laughed. "We can get all the power we want without touching the lake. The natural flow's enough."

"And you can pay your bills now."

"Better than that." said Saul. He drew one hand across his forehead in a show of relief, rumpling his eyebrows. "We'll be setting up more generators, bigger ones. Come the spring runoff, we should be able to get a couple of megawatts out of the place."

"Ayuh," was all I said. I faded back toward the door, letting others resume the questioning. The papers were going to be full of this for weeks. What would they call it? Escher hydro? Or Klein hydro, for the pun?

Howie dropped in that night. He'd started doing that after my divorce, and he'd kept it up when he found that Bonny didn't mind. We always had the booze on hand, and we never hectored him the way his Emma did. Why he stayed married to her, I didn't know. They had no kids, and she rarely gave him a moment's peace, but whenever she got too mean he would find a way to bring some money home. He worked just enough to keep her with him. The rest of his time was his own.

I fetched him a beer and he followed me back to the living room. He took the rocker near the fireplace. Bonny and I had the easy chairs. She was wearing snub denims and a white blouse. No bra. She knew I liked to watch her, and she catered to me. She didn't seem to mind Howie's appreciative gaze.

I had been telling Bonny what I had seen at the dam. When we had our seats again, I took a pull of my own beer, relit my pipe and recapped for Howie. When I was done, Bonny said, "It sounds like just what we need. If it really works, it should make energy cheaper than ever."

I nodded, Howie said, "Ayuh. Ain't right, though."

"What do you mean?" I asked him.

"What they call a perpetuity machine, eh?"

"You mean perpetual motion," put in Bonny.

Howie shrugged and sipped his beer. "Ain't supposed to be possible."

Perpetual motion wasn't possible. I knew that much physics. So Abby's gimmick wasn't what it seemed. But what was it, then? Where was she getting the power she was producing?

I thought I had a clue that fall, though it didn't make much sense. The Portland paper, one Sunday, carried a small article on the Maine Yankee nuclear plant up to Wiscasset. It seemed their efficiency was off just a hair. They suspected fouling in the steam lines, but the problem was so slight they weren't going to try to fix it until the next scheduled shutdown, next year. They had the Nuclear Regulatory Commission's blessing on that plan.

I tried to connect Maine Yankee with Gerder's gimmick, but all I got was a headache, worse than when I tried to play chess. The connection, if there was one, was anything but obvious. I let it go and went hunting with Howie. The firewood business was quiet — I'd sold out, and the cutters were piling up their logs in the woods for later delivery — and so was the town. I had time for a change, time to chase partridge, rabbit, and deer, time to work on the house and loaf with Bonny.

It didn't last, of course. Folks began to argue over how much sand the roads should get this winter, with the traffic down. The state decided it could no longer afford to subsidize heating fuel for the poor and elderly. The fishermen's cooperative started lobbying for a zoning change so they could build a canning plant. It took time, but I handled it all. I talked the zoning board into giving the co-op its variance, persuaded the hardware stores to put tire chains on sale, and convinced the wealthier townsfolk to take in families who ran out of fuel. I also promised to help a bit myself, by selling what fuel oil I had at cost.

It all worked out. The roads stayed passable, and nobody froze to death that winter. I stayed busy, but spring did come, and with it word that Maine Hydro was now putting out two and a half megawatts.

I didn't believe it. There was no way Bottle Pond could provide enough flow for that much power. The watershed wasn't that big, and even with the spring runoff the outlet stream was just too small. I had to go see.

When I got there, the first thing that struck me was the powerhouse. It was bigger now, and the twist didn't seem so bad, perhaps because the water flowing over its surface was so much deeper. There was turbulence on the roof, waves and swirls and eddies, but through it I could make out four humps that had to mark the generators. The water was ripping down the penstock, through the turbines, back through the fourth dimension, and over the powerhouse, accelerating for another trip through the machinery. The flow from the tailrace seemed oddly small.

The lot held a small truck with Maine Hydro on the side and a red Toyota. I found out who the import belonged to when I entered the office. There was a stranger there, short, stocky, brown eyes surrounded by good-humored crinkles. He wore a hat with a press card in the band. He was talking with Abby and Saul. There was no crowd this time.

Abby waved a hand at me as I entered. "Bruce Hertz," she said. "From the Bangor Daily News. Mayor Bowen."

Hertz gave me a grin, a practiced appraisal, and turned back to where the news was. "I can't say I understand it all," he said. "But you did say the usual hydro plant couldn't get more than a hundred and fifty kilowatts out of this stream?"

"Quite right," Saul nodded.

"And you are getting twenty times that?"

"About," said Abby.

"By using the fourth dimension?"

"It's as if the water falls downward from the outlet of the turbine to the inlet. It's a matter of recycling."

"It falls up?" He looked confused. I couldn't say that I got it either.

"No, no," said Abby. "It falls through the fourth dimensional segment of the Klein bottle. And the way we have it set up, that's always down."

He still didn't get it. Neither did I. But I could see that however they'd rigged it, they were indeed producing power. The dials on the wall were reading high, and the floor, even this far from the generators, quivered under my feet. I had to believe, though I also had to agree with Howie that it didn't seem quite right.

I hung around after Hertz had left with his story. I quizzed Abby and Saul myself, then. Recycling was all well and good, I told them, but you can't get energy out of nowhere. Where was their power coming from? Why was the fourth dimension all downhill? What energy source could they be tapping to accelerate all that water for another run through the turbine?

Eventually, Abby began to look uncomfortable. She turned to Saul for support, doodled on the edge of a blueprint. I kept up the pressure until she finally admitted the truth. "I don't know, Harry. I just don't know. I put this thing together and found out what it did. Why it does it, I just don't know."

So. I went home. I thought about it. I spent the next two months trying to see through the fog of apparent magic, but I didn't know that much physics. I didn't get anywhere. And then Jason was kidnapped.

I had just seen the FBI's agent-in-charge out the door. He'd had no progress to report, though his men and the cops had combed the woods, searched abandoned buildings, and questioned everyone who had ever complained about the dam. Now they were widening their net, looking for known criminals in the area, querying informers as far away as New York, and all the rest that goes with a full-blown kidnap investigation. The agent-in-charge was not hopeful.

When he was gone, Louise stuck her head in the office. I looked up at her and said, "Yes?"

"There's another appointment, Mayor." I scowled. It wasn't in my book. She looked uneasy and added, "He called while you were busy. A General Murphy."

I started to ask her when this general would get here, but even as I opened my mouth, I could hear the door behind Louise. She turned her head, said, "This must be them," and vanished. A moment later, she ushered three men into the office. One of them was clearly the general. He wore a uniform with stars over the beef of authority. He was of middle height, thick-waisted and bullet-headed, and his eyes were metallic slits, as if he had just left a battlefield.

I nodded at him as politely as I could. "General Murphy." I looked at the other two. The general introduced them as they all took chairs. Isaac Glynn was from the NRC, a nondescript young man in an expensive Washington suit. Walter Pooler, a little older and with the intent affability of a salesman or a manager, was from Maine Yankee.

I sat on my surprise and let the general talk. "I represent the Department of Defense," he said. He held a thick packet of identification toward me. I ignored it. "I'm hoping you can help us with a problem. You may have seen a news story awhile ago, about the nuclear plant in Wiscasset losing power."

So that was it. I could almost guess the rest, but I kept silent while Pooler picked up the thread. "It's grown worse lately. We're down almost half a percent, more than two megawatts."

I said something about scale in the pipes, gremlins in the generators. Pooler just shook his head. "It's more fundamental than that, Mayor Bowen. Something is interfering with the core, with the nuclear reactions. We've pinned it down that far." He looked uncomfortable, as if he wasn't used to discussing things he knew weren't possible.

Glynn shifted his weight from hip to hip. He said, "But there's no shortage in the net. Something is compensating for the shortage."

"Something, hell!" the general burst out. "It's this Maine Hydro dam. We've tracked it that far."

"True," said Glynn. "At least we think so. And we don't want to shut Yankee down if we can help it. We were hoping you could ask them to turn things off long enough to see what happens."

I thought about it while I rummaged for pipe and tobacco, loaded and tamped and lit. I puffed smoke into the air. "And if they are responsible?" I finally asked, looking from one to another of my guests.

"Then they'll have to shut down permanently," said Pooler. "Though there should be plenty of other uses for their Klein bottle thing."

The general turned to Pooler with a glare. It seemed he had said too much. Or just enough, with a general in the room, to make me think. After a moment, I said, "I suppose it might stop an A-bomb. Or stifle a Russian reactor. Or. . . ." I stopped when the general began to redden. "I suppose it won't hurt to ask them to shut down. Do you think this might have anything to do with the kidnapping?"

Glynn looked puzzled, but Pooler was a Mainer. He knew what was happening. So did the general. He said, "We've been assuming that, and we don't want the secret used for a ransom. As soon as they agree to cooperate, we'll bring in the CIA. Since they keep track of foreign agents, it shouldn't take long. I'm told they already have a good idea of where to look."

"Saul and Abby will cooperate," I said. "Let's go."

When we reached the dam, we found Howie already there, talking to Abby. They broke off as we entered, and Howie grinned at the men and the uniform behind me. "Looks like I'm just a hop ahead of you, Mayor," he said.

"What do you mean?" I asked, puzzled.

"He thinks a spy's got Jason," said Abby. Her eyes were puffy, but her voice was as firm as ever. I looked at Howie, but he wouldn't elaborate. "Do you?" she added.

I nodded. "It could be. We'll know more if you'll turn the generator off for a few minutes."

She didn't like the idea, but when Pooler explained why, she agreed immediately. She used the same knife-switch as before. Pooler then used the phone to call Wiscasset. We listened to him ask, "What's the shortfall now, Jim?" We heard the relief in his voice when he said, "And it should stay that way." And as he hung up, we heard Abby's anger. "What do you mean, 'Stay that way'? We have a living to make!"

"But Mrs. Wilkins . . ." said the general. "It's interfering. . . ."

"How?" she cried. "And why Maine Yankee?"

Trust Howie to spot a layout. "Where it's aimed," he said. "South-southwest."

We checked a map on the wall, and he was right. The stream pointed right at Wiscasset, the penstock paralleled the stream, and the turbines were dead in line with both. I wondered about the model — that hadn't been bolted down — but I kept my mouth shut. Let the experts worry about that, I told myself.

Aloud, I said, "Think of it as a better way to get power out of a reactor, Abby. You can't lose."

Jason was home two days later, but it wasn't the CIA that found him. Howie did it. His thoughts of spies had led him to look for strangers. He hadn't found any who weren't on our side, but he had found a sailboat in the harbor, anchored alone and untended for the past month, and before the season at that. He had borrowed a dingy and boarded, at night, and found boy and spy asleep.

As for the rest of the story, the classified lid went on so tight it was months before I learned it all. It took that long for Abby and Saul to be pumped clean and get back to town. They'd been warned to keep their mouths shut, but they both figured that didn't apply to me.

According to Abby, the scientists had had a field day. They had it figured now that her "dimensionalizer" drew on the force that holds the atomic nucleus together. Direction and range were controlled by the circuitry, and it would produce energy as long as nuclear reactions were going on someplace in the neighborhood of the focus.

It therefore solved the energy crisis, since it could be used to tap the sun directly.

"Fat chance," I told her. "Give those brasshats a choice of saving the country with a secret weapon and saving it with cheap power, and I know what they'll go for."

She shook her head and smiled, wearily. "No," she said. "It took some talking, but there'll be sealed units, guaranteed tamper-proof, for every utility in the country. We'll have the power, and they'll have the weapon."

"I'll bet they were tempted to become a utility themselves," I said. "But what do you get out of it?"

Saul brightened at that, but only slightly. "We're permanent consultants," he told me. "As long as we stay away from dams."

For a moment, I sympathized. I didn't imagine they could travel much either, but they'd live, and live well. And I thought of myself. Oil was almost gone, and so was my oil dealership. Now energy promised to be cheap, and I'd lose the firewood business. And being Mayor didn't pay.

What was *I* going to do?

Could the units be made small enough for houses? Cars?

Alas, Poor Yorick

The world is full of ghosts, of myths and legends and bogeymen. Most are mere stories, vaporings of idle minds, but some are real. Real enough to touch and talk to.

We found one of them last fall. We tracked it down, brought it home, and domesticated it. We gave it a name and a home and a place in the community. We even put it on welfare, and none of the folks in our town thought we were coddling it. Ghosts must be laid, after all, even at the price of a little public funding.

The trouble is that ghosts don't stay laid. This one was no exception. It came back to life as soon as Mike Gibbons showed up again. He's a Boston anthropologist who comes down here every spring for the fishing. He had thick black hair once, though he's losing it now. Enough of it's gone so he has to wear either sunburn lotion or a hat on his head, and the rest is well on its way to white. His face is so cracked and crannied that it might be a map of the Near Eastern countries he does his work in. His body, naturally enough, is that of an aging ditchdigger, a layer of fat over plenty of muscle, thick in the middle, burly arms and legs. He's tall, too, half a head over me.

I suppose Mike must wear a suit in Boston, when he's teaching or having tea with the university president, but I've never seen him in anything but suntans. Working clothes. Fishing clothes. He was wearing them when he came by my office the other day. When Louise showed him in, her voice held a paradoxical tone, as if she were simultaneously sniffing at his inelegance and fawning over his title. "Professor Gibbons," she said, holding the door for him. "He would like a few minutes, Mayor."

She'd have made anyone else wait, suntans or suit. But she knew I wasn't busy, no appointments, not much paperwork, and a *Professor* should never have to cool his heels. That was Louise. A snob, who thought she could surely run the town better than me. At times, I wished she were right. She would certainly be more decorative in the job.

I waved him to a seat, asked him what was up, and picked up my pipe. It had gone out, so I relit it. As the smoke billowed over my desk, Mike said, "I've been fishing the river, Harry. Up by the new bridge. Above the falls. And I saw something strange."

I could guess what he'd seen. The new bridge — new in '79, that is — carried the Doak Road over the river, and just up the road. . . . But I pushed the buzzer, and when Louise stuck her head in the door, I said, "Coffee, please. We'll be a little while." Then I let him go on.

"Fellow on a rock, with a spear. He was getting fish, too. I envied him." Hunched in the chair, he shook his head. His mouth had a rueful twist, and I thought him still impressed by the memory. Though not necessarily by the fisherman's skill. He could do as well, I knew.

"They're good at that," I said.

"All of them? I followed him home when he was done. Tried to speak to him, but he didn't seem to understand a word. Though he didn't object to me tagging along."

"Led you to the farm, did he?"

Mike nodded. "Rundown place, isn't it? No animals except a dog or two. No crops. And two dozen adults and children running around half naked."

"Ayuh. You meet Ngkurkha?"

"The one who speaks English?" He leaned forward in his seat and nodded again. "So that's his name. He sent me to you when I started asking questions. And I should have known you were involved."

"That's what we told him to do when we gave 'em the farm. Gives me a chance to block publicity."

His lean steepened. He braced his palms on his knees. His face wrinkled as he almost glared at me. "You mean you're trying to keep this secret? They should be on a reservation somewhere! Where they can be studied. Protected! Not parked on a farm out in the boondocks to rot."

I waved my pipe at him, but before I could speak, the door opened. Louise brought two mugs in. She looked like she wanted to stay and listen, but I shooed her out and found the sugar and imitation cream in one of my desk drawers. Then I said, "Take it easy, Mike. That's not our way here, and you know it. The farm gives them shelter, the woods and river give them the food they're used to, the way they like it, the warden won't bother 'em, and we see to it they get some extra food. Get a doctor out to 'em, too, once in a while."

"But, but. . . ."

"And they don't need any other kind of protection as long as no one knows they're there."

"But the future! You can't just park them on a preserve forever!"

"Don't intend to. We're giving them a hand until they learn the language and the ways. Then they should fit right in. Already, we've got dockworkers over to Searsport no prettier."

He was quiet for a moment. He settled back in his seat and took a swallow of coffee. He stared out the window. Then he said, "It makes sense, I guess, though some folks think assimilation is a dirty word. But it's such a waste. If you keep them secret, no one will ever know what they're like. No one will ever be able to study them."

That had never been our intention. All we wanted was to give them a chance to adapt at their own pace, unpressured. I told him so, studying him as I spoke. I had known Mike for years, and I trusted him as much as I did any man. And I knew from watching him in the woods and around town that he was a sympathetic observer, unobtrusive despite his bulk, friendly, and willing to pitch in where extra hands were needed. Finally, I added, "Why don't you do the studying? Since you know the secret anyway."

His face lit up. The wrinkles smoothed away and the eyes glowed. I might have offered a historian a time machine. He said, "Students, too?" A practical historian.

"Sure," I said. "But do keep it under your hat for a year or two. Give 'em a chance to settle in."

He nodded his agreement. "Seems fair. But you'll have to tell me. . . ."

"How they got here? Of course. How about tonight? Care to join Bonny and me for supper?"

Bonny was my wife. My second wife. She had been my secretary before the divorce and for a few years after, but she'd quit after the wedding. I'd regretted that ever since. For one thing, it had let Louise in. For another, I could no longer watch my Bonny all day, and that had always been a pleasure. I missed her intelligence and competence as well.

We lived in an old white farmhouse a little outside of town. The apple trees out back were covered in blossoms now, and the daffodils were up. Eight cords of logs, next winter's heat, were piled in the driveway, the lawn mower, an old push-pull reel number, parked beside them. Mike's junior pickup was already there when I got home, pulled to one side to give me room to get into the garage.

He met me at the walk, and we went in the kitchen door together. We found Bonny at the counter, slicing carrots, looking domestic in a little apron of yellow toweling. As she turned to greet us, I stroked her dark hair and collected a kiss. Mike stared. "Pretty as ever," he said as she held out a hand. "You should have come to Boston instead of here. Then I'd have had a chance."

She grinned and said, "It's good to see you again, Mike. Blarney and all. What are you feeding the kids these days?"

"Same old stuff. Though it looks like that could change now."

"He's found the farm," I said as he flicked his eyes around the room, looking for a chair. There were three by the table, on the other side of the wood stove. I pointed one out to him. "Want a drink?"

Whcn he nodded, I fetched the bottles from the cupboard and got glasses and ice. Bonny said, "He would," and turned back to her carrots. "Just wine for me."

"Ayuh." I poured scotch for Mike and me. "I told him he could study them as long as he kept his mouth shut."

"And he agreed?" She paused, thinking. "Though it'll take a while to do the studying, won't it?"

"At least a year," Mike answered her. "Probably more. And I don't want a lot of competition here." He took the glass I handed him and sipped. He raised it to me with a glance of appreciation. It was a fair single-malt, smokier and more mellow than any blend could be. "I'll be quiet at least until I'm ready to publish. Maybe longer if they still aren't ready for the exposure."

"Good man," I said.

"He just wants to stay on our good side." Bonny smiled as she made the accusation. "If he doesn't mess it up, it'll do his reputation more good than the Hittites ever did."

Mike nodded and grinned. She was right, after all. "Though Harry did promise to tell me how he found them."

"After supper," I said.

Once we'd eaten, suffering through the need to talk about anything but the farm and its occupants, about the fishing, the weather, being an unpaid small-town mayor, digging for history, university politics, and all the rest, we took our coffee into the living room. Once we were settled in comfortably and I had a low fire built in the grate, I started to talk. Mike never interrupted, though after a few minutes he did fish a notebook out of his hip pocket and begin taking notes with a worn stub of a pencil.

For years, I began, Waldo County has enjoyed the reputation of a good place to hunt for deer. Every fall, the kill is among the biggest in the state. But, last year and the year before, the kill was off. No one had a guess on the why of it, either. The previous winter hadn't been particularly bad, the coyotes hadn't come this far south and east in any numbers, and the kills hadn't been any greater than usual in the years before. The deer just weren't there — at least, they weren't being fetched to the tagging stations.

Not that the hunters gave up. Every one of them believed the deer were there and that his (or, a very small sometimes, her) luck or skill would find them. Howie Wyman and I were no exceptions.

Howie's an old friend of mine, as Mike knew well enough. He'd shown Mike more than one place to find trout, and Mike liked the man, for all his scruffiness. Howie habitually wore battered work boots, dirty overalls, a checked flannel shirt, and a floppy green felt hat. When he went hunting, he made one concession to the game laws by replacing the hat with a fluorescent — "hunter" — orange cap. He added a coat, too, depending on the weather, but that was just as disreputable as the rest of his outfit, a faded khaki parka, filled with down and covered with pockets. Hc looked like he knew his way around the woods, and he did. After all, he spent every minute he could spare fishing and hunting, escaping from his nagging wife and her need for money. He even had a guide's license, though money generally meant odd jobs for him.

It was nearly the end of the season, Thanksgiving two days away, and neither of us had so much as seen a deer. There hadn't even been much sign. For that reason, we welcomed the thin snow that had fallen the night before, and we headed for a spot Howie knew. "It's well off the roads," he told me. "Good hour's hike 'round Frye Mountain. But the deer are always there."

I hoped he was right, but throughout our hike we saw only two tracks, and they were half full of snow. Night tracks, and not fresh. Even rabbit sign was scarce.

We hunted for hours. We stood still, waiting and listening, hoping a deer would break the silence. We stalked the slopes of the mountain, stumbling over rocks and clefts, disturbing the powdery snow, hoping to spook a buck into its leaping run. But we found nothing. Few tracks, no snorts in the brush, no puffs of steam, no flags, even in the distance. The deer just weren't there.

Toward the end, as the overcast sky darkened with the fall sunset, we rested on an outcropping of the mountain's granite. We brushed the snow away, set our butts on rock, and sighed. I lit my pipe. Howie wadded a chew of tobacco into his cheek. Neither of us said a word. We didn't need to.

Idly, Howie kicked at a rock on the ground before us. It rolled, oddly light, shed its mantle of snow, and grinned at us.

"By time!" swore howie. "Somebody caught it, sure!"

"Ayuh," I said. I leaned my rifle on our rock and bent to pick the skull up. "Shot, too." I pointed to the small hole below one cheekbone and the larger one in the opposite temple.

"Not lately, though." He was right. The skull, nearly as bleached as an anatomist's prop, bore numerous signs of a porcupine's gnawing attentions, though it did retain a fcw raveled tags of gristle. Hairs were stuck to it as well, long, straight, and coarse.

"Some poor hunter," said Howie. "Got taken for a deer. Happens too damned often."

"Ayuh." I stooped and stirred around in the litter at our feet. I found more bones, a piece of an upper arm, most of the pelvis, a handful of fragments. There was no trace of clothing, no buckles or buttons, no shells or guns or knives. No hunter's orange. I snorted in disgust.

"Whoever it was must have stripped him."

"'Less he was naked in the first place."

"Hah." I snorted again.

"Don't laugh. I've heard tales."

"What kind of tales?"

He spat a stream of dark tobacco juice into the snow. "You know. And look." He pointed at the skull. "It ain't your usual head."

He was right, again. As I examined it more carefully, I saw the wisdom teeth, the receding chin, the heavy brows, the odd bulge at the rear. With a little imagination, I could put flesh back where it had been. "He couldn't have been any too handsome. Not that it matters. We'll have to take this back."

"Give it to the sheriff?"

"Of course." I handed the skull to Howie with a grimace. "Here. You'vc got bigger pockets. I can handle the rest of this."

We left with the skull bulging out the game pocket in the back of Howie's parka, the pelvis swinging from my left hand, the other bones filling my pockets. I wondered at the time if I would be able to stand to wear my coat again. I didn't expect Howie to have any such trouble.

The sheriffs office was next door to the town hall, in an old brick building that should have been condemned years ago. As it was, neither the state nor the county could afford to build a new jail. They were even hard put to it to keep the plaster patched and the pipes painted, and while the prisoners didn't complain about their cramped, dim cells, the do-gooders did. The sheriff, Ben Quimby, figured he didn't need to worry about the bitching until his charges managed to push a wall down and escape. Nobody wanted to bet they wouldn't do it one of these days, but so far the closest any of them had come was the fellow who popped the bars out of the crumbling mortar of his window. He'd gone downstreet for a pizza and a beer and been back before morning.

Ben was a small, slim fellow who wore a delicate line of hair on his upper lip, kept his badge buffed and his holster polished, and favored knife-edge creases in bis trousers. He liked to look sharp, and he knew he did.

When Howie and I showed up in his office, he was reading the latest *Playboy*, feet up on his desk. "Put the tits away, Ben," I said. "We've got business for you."

"Hah!" he said. "They've got a lady sheriff this month. See?" He held the magazine up and let it unfold for us. We saw. The badge, as shiny as his, didn't cover much. "But what you got'"

Howie bent his arm around to get at his game pocket. I dropped the pelvis on Ben's desk, beside his left boot. He jerked the boot away and sat up. Howie got the skull loose and held it up. I started fishing the rest of the bones out of my pockets. "My God!" said Ben. "Where'd you get all that?"

"Up on Frye Mountain," I said.

"Some hunter," said Howie. "Year or two ago by the look of him."

"We have not had any disappearances," said Ben.

I shrugged. "Maybe he wasn't reported missing. Maybe nobody knew he was here. Out-of-stater."

"Shee-it," said Ben. "I should have known it was too quiet around here."

"Means you and the chief are doing your jobs," I said. "That's the way we like it."

"Ayuh. So now I've got to go dig up the coroner."

"You'll let me know what he says?"

Ben eyed the remains again, licked his lips, and waved an arm. "Don't know why, Mayor, but sure. Give you a copy of his report, even."

"Fine." We turned, leaving the bones on his desk. At the door, I glanced back. Ben had the *Playboy* in onc hand, staring at it. But duty called. He dropped the magazine and reached for the phone.

I had the report a week later. As soon as I'd read it through, I had Louise call Howie and tell him to drop by for a drink that night.

He showed up about nine. I let him in, shoved a drink in his fist, and set him down at the kitchen table. Then I waved the report at him. "That fellow wasn't a hunter, Howie! The coroner figured it out."

"What are you talking about?" asked Bonny. "What hunter?"

I looked at her, standing in front of the fridge, her own drink in her hand. I'd forgotten I hadn't told her what we'd found. "Didn't want you to worry, honey. But when we went hunting the other day, well, we found somebody's bones."

Her eyes widened, but she didn't say a word. I went on. "And the coroner says they aren't old enough."

"Old enough?" said Howie. Bonny looked puzzled too.

"Ayuh. What with no fillings and the shapes of the things, he says they're too new to be what they look like. Because that skull should belong to a Neanderthal."

"But they were in Europe, and Asia," said Bonny. "Forty thousand years ago."

"Ayuh," I said. "But that's what he said. And I believe him. He's a bright fellow, just out of school, and, besides, he put a picture of a real Neanderthal skull in the report." I held it out to Howie. Bonny stepped around until she could see too.

"Dead ringer, ain't he," said Howie. "Not so fresh, though. And nobody's seen them."

"So they stay out of sight, hole up in hunting season, when folks are in the woods. Except for one. Maybe they come out at night, and he got jacked."

"Might be why the deer are scarce," offered Howie.

"I suppose," I said. "Might have moved in here just a couple years ago."

"Too crowded down south."

Bonny nodded at that and drained hcr glass. "It would be nice to see them," she said.

"Ayuh," I said. "But we'd have to find 'em first."

"I can do that," said Howie. "Now we know they're there."

"How long'd it take you?"

He shrugged. "A day. A year. Depends how good they are at hiding sign."

I left it at that. I thought he might be bragging, but I surely didn't want to stop him trying. Just as well I didn't say anything, too, for a week later Howie joined me at the diner for lunch and said he'd done it. Did I still want to see 'em? Tomorrow?

Tomorrow it was. Howie drove Bonny and me up to Frye Mountain, took a track through the woods I hadn't seen before, parked his pickup, and led us off on foot. We walked for almost an hour, our feet crackling through leaves and twigs, scuffing the patches of unmelted snow. We smelled the tang of distant woodsmoke, heard the silence, broken only by the occasional squirrel and a rare blast of a shotgun. The deer season was over, and with it went the rattling of rifles, but now the rabbit season was with us. "'Cept the bunnies ain't there neither," said Howie.

The hike, pleasant as it was, had to end sometime. I noticed we were headed for a bluff, a shoulder of the mountain marked by boulders nnd ledge. There was a low rise between us and it, and Howie halted us just before we could see over it. "They're in the hollow just ahead," he said. "In caves. So belly down, now." We did as he said and crawled the rest of the way, as quietly as we could, though our noise — even Howie's — seemed loud to me.

When we reached the top of the rise, there was a thin screen of brush before us. The branches were leafless and we could see, but I didn't think we could be seen. And there they were. The caves, no more than clefts in the rock, backed a scatter of ugly figures. They were knot-featured, heavy-browed, short, and hairy. They wore no clothes, despite the December weather, and their feet were flat and strikingly large.

"How many?" I whispered.

Howie shrugged as best he could in his position. "Dunno. Some could be in the caves. Or hunting."

"Poor things," said Bonny. "They shouldn't have to live like this."

"It's all they know," I said. "We haven't been any better off for very long, ourselves."

"I know," she said. "But. . . ."

At that moment, there was a soft crackle behind us. We all rolled over to look, and we found ourselves facing a pair of the cavemen. Men, too, all too obviously. Their expressions were stolid, watchful, with no hint of menace. Still, a thrill chased down my back, and by Bonny's shudder beside me I knew she felt something similar. They each held a stone-tipped spear, and when they gestured with their weapons toward the hollow, we rose to obey.

When we came into view, the women and children dashed for the caves. The men gathered, spears in hand, to meet us. As we approached, we began to detect odors — this tribe clearly knew nothing of latrines, much less soap and water — and one of the men stepped forward.

He wasted no time. As soon as we were within speaking distance, he said, "Who you?" His voice was harsh, and his features seemed less clearly Neanderthal. I looked around and saw that the men varied. Their faces ranged from almost pure apeman to nearly human. I wondered if there had been some interbreeding over the years. With Indians, perhaps, or even whites.

When I didn't answer right away, he repeated his question, this time with a jab of his spear toward my belly. I answered him then, as civilly as I could. I told him we were hikers and had found them by accident. When he seemed to understand, I added, as ingenuously as I could manage, "Do you all speak English?"

At that, he laughed and turned to his fellows. He spoke to them in a guttural, barking tongue. When he was done he told us, "Me Ngkurkha. Me listen hunters good, learn plenty. You got whiskey?"

So English wasn't all he learned from our orange-coats. I shook my head as Bonny said, "But perhaps we could get you better shelter, better food."

He grunted and turned away to speak to his fellows again. There was a brief outburst of barks and growls, and this time they all laughed. When he turned back, it was only to gesture at the two behind us and say, "Ngkurkha people got plenty. You no come back. Go!"

We left. Unarmed, we weren't about to argue, even with spears. Besides, we had seen as much as we wanted. The Neanderthals existed, we knew where they were, and if they wanted their privacy, we would leave them alone, at least until we had some notion of what we should do.

We didn't say much to each other till we were back in the truck, and then it was all of the "Did you see. . . ?" variety. I remarked on the deftly flaked spear-points and the lack of visible fire, Howie on their silence in the crackly woods, Bonny on their filth and thinness. By the time we were rolling again, though, we had distance enough to think about what our discovery meant. "We can't leave them there," I said. "We need the game for the tourists, and we need the tourists' money."

"You can't move 'em into town," said Howie. "No way. They wouldn't take it. Too different."

"We have to do something," said Bonny. "We can't just let thern suffer like that."

"They're not suffering," I told her.

"Happy as clams in mud," said Howie.

"It's all they know," I said.

And then we were home. As Bonny put the coffee on, she said, "But we do have to do something. Don't we? If only to take the pressure off the deer. And we can't just chase them out."

"Hate to see a war get going 'tween them and the hunters," said Howie. "Ain't sure who'd win." He paused, chewing his lip as if thinking something over. "I know a social worker who can keep her mouth shut about food stamps."

"I'll bet you do." I was getting the cups out. As I set them on the kitchen table, I added, "But that's not such a bad idea. Get them some regular food, show them how to use latrines or toilets, start them learning how we live."

"Ayuh. Maybe even get 'em a better place to live, like Bonny told 'em."

"Come to think of it," I said. "The town owns that old farm on the Doak Road. Got it for the taxes, and no one's bid on it yet at auction."

"Out of the way," said Howie. "A wreck. Pa'tridges in the orchard, though."

I nodded. "Woods all around, the river close by, they could keep up some hunting, too."

"But wouldn't the warden object?" asked Bonny. "I'm sure they wouldn't understand about bag limits and closed seasons."

"Get 'em Indian licenses. Natives, ain't they?"

The coffee was ready. Bonny poured it and we sat down. Then she said, "If they'll move in, I suppose that means they'll have more contact with the rest of us."

"Ayuh," I said. I pulled my pipe from my pocket and began to stoke it. "They'll all learn English. By the time the kids are grown, they should fit in pretty well."

"Have to fix the place up a bit," said Howie."

"Not much, not for them," I said. When Bonny began to look offended, I went on, "Clean the chimney, check the plumbing, get 'em a stove and a woodpile. Furniture and paint, they won't even want for a while, not after living in caves."

"You want to talk to the warden?" asked Howie. "He don't care for me much." I didn't wonder why. I nodded and said I'd see to the fix-up too, as long as he would try to talk Ngkurkha around. I wasn't particularly eager to face those spears again, myself.

And so it went. The place was ready in a month, and by then Howie had talked Ngkurkha into taking a look at it. The man, if he was really that, wasn't terribly impressed, but he did recognize the value of decent shelter. He checked the woods for game sign, looked the river over, and sampled the supplies we'd laid in. Then he grunted and told Howie to take him home.

He didn't come back right away. In fact, he might never have moved in if we hadn't had an early cold snap, frigid enough to freeze the equipment right off any man without a proper set of thermal underwear. He came then, all right, and when Howie checked the place just after New Year's, he found a roaring fire in the stove and apemen all over the place. Each one had staked out his or her own patch of floor, and the hotshots were all in the kitchen, close to the heat.

When I was done, Mike grunted and laid his notebook down. Bonny said, "They took it pretty well. No one's left, and I'm sure their lives are easier now."

"Their lives are still mostly their own, too," said Mike. "We — I mean civilization, anthropologists, soldiers, the works — we've messed up enough primitives already. You've got this bunch under your eye, but you're not forcing them. Not much, anyway."

"We did want to give them a chance," I told him. "To settle in as much their own way as our presence allows. But it'll be a while before we get shoes on them."

Mike raised his eyebrows. "How so?"

"I told you they had big feet. They may even be the Big Foot itself. The Sasquatch. Twice the size of mine." I propped a boot on one knee and let him look at it.

"But what's the problem?"

"Have you ever seen a size 24 shoe?"

Return of the Native

Our town is generally a quiet, peaceful place. There is little crime and less controversy. Politics is marked mainly by its unanimity, and the great issues of the day rarely touch us deeply. But we do have a few creative citizens with a knack for disturbing the peace. We also have a history that every few years throws up an echo to relieve the quiet.

This time — well, Bonny and I were at home, in the old, white farmhouse I've owned for years. We were in the living room, having coffee by the woodstove I'd plugged into the fireplace back when oil first went dear. Neither one of us was wearing much, which prompts me to say that wood heat is vastly underrated. Sure, it's cheap and it's personal, but it is also luxurious. You just can't bask in front of a radiator or a hot air vent. And when you are married to a dark-haired lovely, your ex-secretary, of remarkable intelligence, sympathy, and competence, you like to bask.

But that is really neither here nor there. We were having coffee, playing at backgammon, being snug amidst January cold and snow. We were talking, too, trying to decide whether we wanted children in our lives. We were no closer to a decision than ever when we were interrupted by a distant screen of sirens.

I wondered what was up. Bonny said, "You could call, you know. They'd tell you."

I allowed as how they probably would. We listened as the sirens faded. They hadn't gone on too long, so whatever it was couldn't be far from the station. Probably right in town. I got to my feet, belted my robe, and headed for the phone in the kitchen. I called the station and got the Chief. I told him what I wanted, and he said, "The Hutchison place, Mayor. Mrs. Morse across the street reported a scream."

I thanked him and hung up. It could have been a burglar, a wife-beater, or just a nightmare, but I didn't ask why they'd used the sirens. Jack Hutchison was a councilman and the head of the school board, after all.

The next morning I went to my town hall office. There were papers to tend to, calls to make, people to see, all the busywork of being Mayor. And none of it was welcome, really. The job was unpaid, and I barely knew why I kept running. Perhaps it was that I felt needed, by everyone except my secretary. Louise had replaced Bonny after the wedding, and she was a poor trade. For one thing, she felt sure she could run the town just fine without me.

The head of the Chamber of Commerce had just left, having put his case for a traffic light at the new mall. One was needed, but was that enough reason to bring in the first of the things? The town was small, and so far we had avoided them, except for a yellow blinker at Main and High. Most folks seemed to like it that way.

The door opened again a minute after he had left. I glimpsed Louise's backside moving my way, heard her saying, "You can't just barge in!" and spotted an old friend trying to get past her. "Hey, Howie!" I called. "C'mon in."

Louise stopped, turned around, and smiled. "But he doesn't have an appointment," she complained.

"He doesn't need one," I told her. "You should know that by now."

She sniffed again, but she moved aside. The other pushed past her none too gently. Howie Wyman. Overalled, felt-hatted, work-booted. As grubby as a laborer, not that he worked unless he had to. He was the town loafer, dedicated to fishing and hunting above all else. And a friend.

With Louise gone and the door closed once more, I waved Howie to a seat. He took it, removed his hat, scratched his grey head, and said, "Keith's back."

I didn't say a thing. I was busy, getting a pipe from my desk drawer, loading it, lighting it. But I was puzzled. I must have shown it, for he added, "Hutchison."

Ah. Now I remembered. The teen-ager who had caught a ride on an interstellar freight train. Lydia Seltzer and I had taken him and another kid up to Pork Hil to look for the wendigo. He and Lydia had found it, too, though Lydia had made it back a mite sooner. I blew smoke and said, "The commotion last night, eh?"

"Ayuh," he nodded. He looked around the floor. I toed my waste basket toward him. He spat a stream of brown tobacco juice. "Saw him at the Diner this mornin'. Said his Ma screamed when he came in. Thought sure he was a ghost."

"And Jack?"

"Happy enough, I guess. His Ma, too, now."

I snorted gently. Like I said at the beginning, history and echoes. I wondered what Keith had been up to all these years — five, was it? — and what he was like now. What had he done and learned? What had he returned for?

Howie spat again. "Did say he had the best night's sleep since he left. Seems they don't use mattresses out there. More like hammocks."

I chuckled, imagining Bonny and myself. "Like to try one, would you?"

He shook his head. "Spent enough summers in 'em." He paused, as if remembering. "Said he'd be in to see you later on."

"Think I'd better tell Louise?"
He laughed. So did I.

I spent the rest of the morning trying to empty my IN box. I didn't succeed, of course — the mail came before I was done, and then I had it all to do over again. I groaned and gave up. My concentration wasn't what it should have been. My mind kept coming back to Keith's return. I kept asking myself what and why, though I knew the questions were pointless until he came by to tell me.

Finally, I checked my watch and decided it wasn't too early for lunch. It would be the Diner. Keith had been there that morning, and perhaps Barbara would have something more to tell me.

Barbara Johnson had run her diner for years, taking over when her father retired and adding organic dishes to the menu. That had attracted the sprouts crowd, though she had kept the standard fare as well. It all was good enough, but her reputation was based firmly on her pies and coffee.

Barbara was taking orders behind the long counter when I walked in. I hung up my coat, took a stool, and stared at the chalkboard full of specials on the wall before me. Within a minute, she stood in front of me. She rattled a cup of coffee onto the counter by my hand and said, "You hear the news, Harry? Keith's back?"

"Howie told me," I said. I looked at her. Bleach-blonde hair threatening to explode from a helmet A strong lined face, a thickening body. She was always smiling, always friendly, always far more attractive than a first glance suggested. And she had never learned to whisper. Everyone in the place must have heard her question. When I turned my head, they were watching, their voices quiet.

"Damn," she said conversationally. "Sometimes I wish I wasn't tied to this counter. Then I could dash across the street and be the first to tell you something for a change." I nodded when she paused to grimace. "Did he tell you how different the boy looks?"

Interested, I said, "No," and asked her what she meant.

She shrugged. "It's hard to say. But different. Like he should be the boss of some big operation. You know why he's here?"

I told her I hadn't seen him yet, though he'd told Howie he was going to drop in. Then I gave her my order and settled in to listen to the crowd. They were talking Keith, Keith, Keith. He had defected to Russia. He had been kidnapped. He had run away to join a circus and had been around the world. He had disappeared in mysterious circumstances and been brought back by a flying saucer. That last was closest to the truth, I knew, and I was surprised that more people didn't seem to recall Lydia Seltzer and Pork Hill.

Louise ushered Keith in early that afternoon. I had spoken to her, but the results astonished me. She acted as if the young man behind her were an ambassador or a millionaire. She was completely out of character, and I was sure it couldn't be due entirely — or at all — to what I'd said.

Then I saw Keith. And he was different, just as Barbara had said. He was only in his early twenties, of course, but he seemed older. He was thin, wiry, browned by strange suns, tall enough to look down on most folks, and he wore an air of maturity, confidence. My first impression was that here was a clearly superior being. I had never felt that way about anyone before. I wondered if the Indians had fell the same when one of their fellows returned from a stay among the whites.

I stared while he took a seat. I stared until he broke the silence with, "Good afternoon, Mayor Bowen." I stared — he was the Keith I remembered, but a new Keith, a not-Keith — and I finally managed, "It's been a long time."

"It has." He smiled reflectively and adjusted a pants leg. The fabric was a light green that matched his shirt and jacket. The cut was strange, and there was an unfamiliar sheen. "I'm sorry I disappeared that night. You must have worried, I know my parents did. But I got too close to the tachtrain's field and . . ."

I waved a hand. "Lydia made it back. She had pictures, so we knew you were all right."I fumbled for my pipe. "And now you've made it back, too. For good? Or just a visit?"

"A visit, I think. The first of many. I've been trained . . ."

"We heard a rumor. Saucer pilot?"

He shook his head, gently. "No. They tend to start new groups off at higher levels than that. A test of responsibility, of potential. A way to give a real sense of participation. I'm a monitor."

Again. I remembered. I'd never met a monitor, but I knew of them. Scanning the cosmos for improbability waves generated by the aliens' contiguity manipulators, devices that let one switch components among the parallel universes, the monitors were the aliens' rescue squad and police. Though not police, exactly. They watched, detected irresponsible switchings, and set things right again.

"Then you have a manipulator?" I asked.

"Of course." It would be implanted in his brain. "Though I'm not really here as a monitor. Not even as a visitor."

"You have a job?" I set my pipe down, interested.

He nodded. "My first real assignment. You might say I'm a trader."

My look conveyed the question. What could we have to trade with an interstellar civilization, a people who had tachtrains and contiguity manipulators? He answered me with words. "The Gerder Tap," he said. "It's an elegant solution to the energy problem. They've got nothing like it. They want it."

"But how?" I asked. "How do you hope to get it? The government has it more tightly classified than the A-bomb was in 1945. They aren't about to give anyone the plans."

He tapped his head with one forefinger and grinned at me. "The manipulator," he said. "There is a certain African dictatorship negotiating with Washington now for nuclear power plants. By the time I'm done shuffling the documents around, it will have Taps instead. And that will open things up for me."

After Keith's disappearance five years ago, the Army had stepped in. It had confiscated Lydia's photos and taken over Pork Hill, and ever since it had been trying to catch another tachtrain. It knew about Keith, too, and it must have heard rumors of his return.

It was less than an hour after Keith had left my office that I had more visitors. A trio of black-suited stonefaces, from Army Intelligence, they said. They wanted to know what I knew of Keith's return.

I told them as little as I could. Yes, I had been visited by a man who claimed to be Keith. But he didn't look much like the Keith I remembered. He might have been an imposter.

"Never mind that" said the tallest of the three. His name, according to his papers, was Kippers, John L. "We want the guy. Where is he?"

When I only shrugged, the second — Fenton, Samuel — said, "We think he could help us with the Pork Hill project. Get us into space at last. What did he want?"

"He was saying hi to old friends. What else?"

"That's what we want to know," said Kippers. He pulled the front of his jacket apart. A pair of handcuffs hung from his belt. "If you won't tell us, we'll have to take you back to the base."

I studied them while the third — I didn't catch his name — told me they'd already seen Keith's parents. I didn't think they could have been much help. I wondered if I would help or hurt Keith's plans by talking. I told myself the government would have to know eventually, and finally I said, "He did say something about being a trader now."

They jumped on that. Kippers almost shouted his next words: "And what's he after here?"

I turned my hands palm up and held them over my desk. "He didn't say. What could we offer an interstellar civilization? The only thing I can think of is the Tap."

They stared at me in silence for a full minute. Then, as one, they turned and left. They didn't even say, "Thanks."

The Gerder Tap had been invented by Abby Gerder, an out-of-stater who had come to town to set up a small hydro-electric plant. The plant's capacity was too small to suit her, though. In order to boost the output, she had devised four-dimensional Klein bottle. The water fell downhill through the fourth dimension from the plant's tailrace to the turbine inlet, a perfect example of recycling. The device had let her go from 150 kilowatts to 2500. It wasn't possible, but it worked and Abby was dreaming of wealth until the feds stepped in. It seemed she was drawing her power from the Maine Yankee nuclear plant up to Wiscasset; perpetual rnotion wasn't possible. They shut her down, studied what she'd done, and soon found out that she'd been tapping nuclear reactions directly. Suddenly, they had a way to snuff an A-bomb, stifle a reactor, or draw power safely and efficiently from the sun. The Gerda Tap, they named it, and it was being integrated into the country's power net as quickly as possible. For security, units were booby-trapped against tampering and spying. And Abby — and her husband — were permanent consultants, quite rich enough to keep their mouths shut.

The government was possessive enough about the Tap that I didn't believe Keith had much of a chance. His manipulator could confuse the paperwork, but I didn't see how he could change official minds or blind the security watchdogs.

Of course, I underestimated the power of paperwork. That became more than clear over the next few months. The headlines told the story, and they told it in away that made me wonder if Keith was even involved:

JAMBEZRI OIL FOR NUKES?
GUERRILLAS SEIZE JAMBEZRI OIL FIELDS
DEFENSE RELUCTANT ON JAMBEZRI NUKES
BOMBERS FREE OIL FIELDS
GATIN ASKS AID TO REBUILD
AMNESTY INTERNAT'L REPORTS JAMBEZRI BLOODBATH
GATIN: ANOTHER AMIN?
EPA SUGGESTS SOLAR TAPS
NO REBELS, SAYS JAMBEZRI PRES
JAMBEZRI THREAT TO PROLIFERATION?
COMMERCE REFUSES NUKE EXPORT
DEFENSE SAYS TAPS COPYPROOF, NO WEAPON
JAMBEZRI TO GET TAPS

That wasn't all of it by a long shot, but it gives the flavor. A ruthless dictator with a resource we needed, less for fuel now than for feedstocks. A trade offered. Worry about giving Gatin a way to build A-bombs. An environmentally benign solution that could never be an offensive weapon. Assurances that the boobytraps made it impossible for anyone to copy a Tap. And the decision.

Since Jambezri was a small country, it didn't take long to get the Taps set up. Within a year, there were Tap-powered desalination plants, irrigation projects, and factories. Within two years, Jambezri was well on itsway to industrialized prosperity. And Gatin was out. With the sudden prospect of plenty, his brand of government, with its graft and monopolization of wealth, was no longer tolerated. His soldiers and police became consumers.

That was when Keith came back to my office. Howie was with me at the time. We were talking about going partridge hunting sometime soon. The season was open, and by all reports it was a good year for the birds, but I was busy. Maybe too busy. My oil business had sunk with all the rest years before, and though I hadhoped to be able to sell Taps for home and car use, they'd been reserved for the utilities. Still, I did a good business in electrical heating systems and in firewood. And with the cold weather coming, I was hopping.

Louise interrupted us with that look of respect I had seen only once before.

I recognized it as soon as her head poked through the opening door, and I said, "Is Keith here?"

She nodded at me. "Mr. Hutchison would like to see you."

"Then send him in." She did, and I took a long look at the young man who had — I guessed — been working miracles in Washington. He seemed no older, though a trifle browner, and his alien clothes had been exchanged for a well-cut blue suit. He wore a tie and carried a slim attache case. He smelled of cologne, too.

I had compared him once with an Indian who had been among whites. Now I did so again. He had an alien education, perhaps alien values as well. But he also knew his native world, its gestalt, and could move among his erstwhile fellows as no alien could. He was the perfect stalking horse, and I wondered if he was just that, just as his like had been again and again in human history. He hadn't done anything I felt shouldn't have been done, but wasn't a monitor supposed to be a paragon of ethical responsibility? Still, could I — could we — trust him not to rip us off?

Howie nodded at him as he found a seat. "Good to see you again," he said. "Still like mattresses?"

Keith gnnned. "I've been back in hammocks since then," he said. "But yes. I do."

"A matter of upbringing," I offered.

"I suppose so," said Keith.

Then I added, "You want to watch out, though, or there'll be some downbringing." When Keith looked puzzled, I told him about the Army men. "They want to pump you if they can."

He thought it over. "I can't allow that," he finally said. "But it's just as well you said what you did. It will help if they're ready when the time comes."

"I s'pose it's best, then," said Howie, "you shouldn't hang around long. Though I was hopin' to hear more about the folks out there."

"There isn't much I can say," the other answered. "To you or the Army. There are rules, you know, and I . . ."

"I understand," I said. "A monitor, especially, must respect the rules."

He nodded. "Besides, there was work to do, and then I had to go back for a time."

"Harry told me somethin' about that work. Seems to have gone all right."

"So far," I said. "But tell me, you can't tell us what it's like out there, I suppose for fear of interfering with our development . . ."

"Something like that," said Keith.

". . . but you're here as a trader. Won't that interfere?"

Keith shifted In his chair. He lost a little of his look of confidence. "Of course it will," he said. "But we need the Tap, and that is more important. Though I am supposed to get it without interfering any more than absolutely necessary."

"Then you should be tryin to steal it," said Howie. "That way you'd get it, and no one here'd know the difference."

He looked still more uncomfortable. He stared at the wall for a moment. Then he said, "True, but we can't do things that way. There must be mutual benefit."

We were silent while I thought over what he'd said. An ethical trader, he had to be. That probably meant both sides had to know there was a trade, too. Finally, I said, "I don't suppose getting rid of one dictator is enough benefit for our side."

He said, "Oh, no. That is only tactics, to make it possible to trade at all." He shook his head. "It's not strictly necessary, perhaps, but this is my first assignment. I want to try the things I was taught."

"Must be more, then," said Howie. "The Tap's still secret."

"There is." Keith lifted his attache case onto his lap and opened it. He extracted a moderately thick stack of white paper and held it out to me. "More tactics," he said.

It was a manuscript. I took it and glanced at the cover sheet. It bore my name. I looked at Keith. "What is this?" I asked.

"You are a mayor, a government official. Someone who might be listened to. I would like you to send this to some journal where it will be read. Perhaps the *Foreign Policy Review*. Its effect will be the next step in my plan."

I hefted the manuscript. I opened it and began to read. The argument was laid out in excruciating detail, far beyond what I was capable of, but in outline it said simply that once exporting the Tap had stabilized one local political situation, it should be made available on a wider scale. It would provide the world with ample, cheap power, lead to universal prosperity, and — the author hoped — foster world peace. As I turned the last page over, Keith said, "The Jambezri case has not been lost on the rest of the world. Despite the political effects, there is great demand for the Taps. Even from the Communist Bloc."

I laid the manuscript on my desk and flattened one hand atop it. "And if this works? If the Taps are spread all over the world? If they do bring peace?"

"Then there won't be much point in secrecy, will there?" Keith grinned.

I sent the manuscript off, of course, and it was published. I didn't doubt it would be, since Keith could influence the content of memos and letters and the like. I wondered that he even needed the manuscript, unless there was no suitable counterpart in some parallel world, though that seemed unlikely. Perhaps this way was just the simplest.

At any rate, it worked. *Foreign Policy Review* is a journal read by statesmen and politicians and State Department bureaucrats. They saw the article, thought about it, discussed it, and in the end decided to ship the Taps — still boobytrapped — wherever they were wanted. In the process, they stirred up the reporters, who wanted to know more about the man responsible for the decision. I let Louise handle them. She was good at that. All I had to worry about was the Army. Its men came back, more than once, though they didn't learn a thing.

The economists helped by pointing out how much the resulting increase in exports would help the nation's balance of payments. I wished they would point out that there was no reason why the Taps couldn't be scaled down to a size that would heat a house or run a car. No reason, that is, except the interests of the utilities and the problem of fitting booby-traps into the smaller units. Electricity was cheap now, so cheap it was heating most homes and powering most cars, but small Taps would improve my business no end. Not that that was the real benefit of the Taps. I'd never dreamed they might result in world peace. Neither had the inventor.

And it actually seemed that they might. As they made energy cheap and plentiful for all, they removed many reasons for war — food, water, resources, even *lebensraum.* There were left only the nastier reasons — nationalism, ideology, religion — and they had been fading for decades. I thought prosperity might make them even less potent.

But how to build a Tap remained a U.S. secret.

I was alone the next time Keith dropped in. Even Louise was away for the day, off visiting friends or family or perhaps getting a little sun at the shore. It was a good day for it, sunny and warm and sweet with the odors of early June. It was such a good day, in fact, that I was planning to knock off early. There was a stream I knew, and a pool that should hold a trout or two, and . . .

But there was Keith, displaying a new tan suit, still brown and confident and superior. He was smiling, too, and when I asked him what he was so pleased about, he said, "I'm almost done now. The Taps are all over the world, there's no more excuse for secrecy, and it's time to trade."

I agreed. "It should be, yes. But the secrecy is still on. They're still boobytrapping every unit. They want to keep a monopoly."

He waved one hand airily. "No problem," he said, with a wider smile. "I can trade with any of a hundred countries, now. I can take a whole Tap home, boobytraps and all, where they'll take it apart and copy it. The booby-traps won't bother our engineers."

"Then why are you here? The Army still wants you."

"They won't for long."

"Why?" His confidence was baffling. In his position, I would have been frustrated by the barriers still facing me, but he, he almost seemed to be ignoring them.

"I would rather have the plans. The Army wants space. If you will get the Pork Hill commander on the phone, we'll both be happy."

I stared at him. Did he think they would be content to talk with him? They would want a full-scale interrogation, with drugs and hypnosis and relays of questioners. Maybe even rubber hoses. I said as much, but Keith only grinned again. "Call," he said. "Tell him I'm offering a faster-than-light starship, together with plans and a list of nearby colonizable worlds. But don't mention the manipulator."

The reminder reassured me. The manipulator would hardly be part of the deal,and with that in his brain, they could hold him only so long as he wished to remain. Locks would fail, I thought. Gas would appear from nowhere. Walls would crumble. And Keith would walk away.

I set my pipe aside and made the call. At mention of my name and title, the corporal on the switchboard passed me immediately to a lieutenant, who gave me a captain, who connected me with Colonel Dickson. All I had to say was that

I had information on the Hutchison case.

Colonel Dickson was more than receptive. He sent a car for us, met us at the door of the quonset hut among the trees at the base of the Hill, and took us to his office. There he sat down behind a broad metal desk, motioned us to chairs, and said, "We've been parked here ever since you disappeared, Mr. Hutchison. We wanted to get one of our men aboard that tachtrain, but yours seems to have been the last to come through."

The Colonel was older than I had expected. Passed-over, perhaps, and given an out-of-the-way assignment. His hair receded above his hornrims, and there were deep lines beside his nose and mouth, lines that told the world how rarely he smiled. At the same time, he was slim, muscular, and he wore his ribboned uniform as well as a store dummy. Keith saw all this as he settled into his seat and adjusted his trouser legs. He said. "I believe they did change the route after I hitched my ride."

The Colonel's laugh was forced. "Then we've wasted eight years. Or have we? After all, we're here when you return. And Mayor Bowen says you want to trade."

I told myself that Keith could as easily have gone directly to Washington. He hardly needed a local intermediary, and I didn't think he would have used one if he hadn't been born and raised here. I didn't say what I thought, though. I merely nodded.

So did Keith. Then he spelled out what he wanted and what he offered. The Colonel's look of greed was unfeigned when he answered. "If it was up to me, you'd have your deal."

"But it's not?"

"Of course not. This'll go all the way to the top. But first, the Pentagon." He pulled out a drawer in his desk and extracted a white telephone. He lifted the receiver and began to talk, without dialing. The line had been open, waiting. After a moment he said, "They want to know where the starship is."

"On the far side of the moon." Keith gave him the coordinates. "It's been there for a month."

"Then it should be on satellite photos." He spoke into the phone again, hung up, and said, "They'll have to check. In the meantime, we have a suite for you."

"We'd rather get back to town," I said. "There's work waiting."

The Colonel didn't want to let us leave, but in the end he had to. We allowed him only one concession, a man to stay with Keith, to see that he didn't disappear again. Not that it mattered to Keith.

The deal went through. How could it fail to? A not-so-secret Tap for a monopoly on interstellar travel. Though the monopoly turned out to be no more than a head start. The U.S. got a working starship, but the very day Keith left with the plans for the Tap, plans for the ship showed up in the capitals of all other nations. Keith was taking no chances on spoiling our progress toward peace.

I don't know why I was surprised at the shape of the starship, but I was. I had expected a flying saucer, a chip from the technological peak of Keith's adopted civilization. But when the news broke, the pictures were of a silvery oblong, battered and dented and scratched with age and use. It was obviously second-hand, obsolete, though it did mean our world's entree into space, a chance to spread out into colonies, to meet our betters on their own ground. It was a seed of the future, but only a seed.

When I thought about it, I realized the truth. Here on Earth, no one hands underdeveloped nations, even those with a few hyperdeveloped brains, the latest in technology. We don't trust babies with loaded guns. Why should those who sent Keith home?

A Love Story

The road his feet walked now was paved, but it was not important enough in the scheme of things to warrant a yellow stripe down its middle. Its blacktop was checkered with cracks and patches. Its camber was warped. Its shoulders slumped into its ditches. It shone with neglect as it wandered among woods and fields and past bedraggled apple trees whose fallen fruit still scented the air.

He wasn't going far. From his house nearer town, he could hear the trucks and cars on the Interstate. From his destination, he would still be able to hear an occasional loud truck. He would see nothing, though, beyond the bare brown canes of berry plants, nets of naked branches against the sky, fading colors in the new-fallen leaves he would scuff along the path.

The path left the road a mile ahead. It skirted a pasture, tunneled through an alder thicket, climbed a wooded hill, and dipped to flank a brook he knew. The big browns bred there. Every fall, they came up from the lake. Fat and lazy, they gathered in the pools, their fins waving like banners, while they chose banks of gravel for their redds.

He had passed there once with a friend. Shotguns in the crooks of their arms, they had been looking for partridge. When they had come to the brook, its banks hung with dry bracken, they had seen the trout. The friend had straddled a small pool, one hardly big enough for the two fish it held, aimed his gun between his legs, and pulled his trigger. Each of them, then, had put a fish in his game bag and prayed they wouldn't meet a warden.

Now he wished to check that brook again. If the fish were there, he might come back at night. He had a thick wool jacket, all red and black in checks, which would protect him against the cold that came when the sun went down. He had a folding net. He had a sucker spear, too, but he thought the net would work the better. Either would offer less risk than a shotgun of attracting a warden's attention.

Too, he wondered if the blight were still there. Last time, near the brook, he and his friend had passed a clearing where nothing grew. That had been two years ago, and he still wondered at it. There had been only stubble where there should have been winter-dead weeds and vines and small trees.

The road was quiet. No cars passed. The few houses he saw were closed in on themselves, smoke drifting from their chimneys. In this season, their residents had no more outdoor chores. Gardens were done for the year. Lawns had finished growing. Firewood was all cut and split and stacked under cover, in woodsheds and garages and basements. A light breeze rattled remnant leaves. The loudest sounds were the whisking of his denimed thighs, the soft clap of his leather boots on the tar.

Yet there was other sound ahead. He heard the chunk of metal on rock, a slosh, an impatient voice. The breeze brought him an odor of foulness. He raised his head, quieted his thoughts, and tried to see past the curve before him, through a tangle of naked lilacs, over a brow of roof and porch.

He rounded the curve. A lawn sloped up to his right. There was a gravel drive just beyond it. Both were carpeted with leaves, golden in the sun, framing a pile of dirt, spade sticking out aslant, a metal wheelbarrow, deep and dripping, and a hole. A woman leaned over the hole, gripping a rope. As he watched, she drew up a bucket and poured its contents, black and viscous, into the barrow.

He left the pavement. He knew the woman, and his nose told him what she was doing. "Afternoon, Miz Jenkins."

She straightened to glare at him boldly. "It's Molly, dammit. I've told you before." She was a tall woman, almost as tall as he, with a glossy black mane and a figure that was defiantly female. She was not beautiful. Her face was too square for that, her lips too thin, her nose too sharp. But her fingers were long and slender, and he had heard her in town, playing the piano and singing her own songs. She had beauty in her.

"Molly," he granted her. He put his hands in his back pockets and leaned on one hip. "Cleaning out the septic tank?"

She gave him a look that said, "You need to ask?" Aloud, she said, "Gotta do it every few years. Last time, Nick took care of it." Like him, like too many of his neighbors lately, she was divorced. He didn't wonder why. There was a plague hereabouts, an infection that sharpened women's tongues and hardened their hearts. His own wife had shown the signs over a year ago. Molly still did, though they had faded since her husband had fled.

"Want a hand?"

She tossed her bucket into the hole again. It clattered against rocks in the soil, perhaps on the rim of the concrete tank itself. It splashed, and drops of sludge joined those already spattering her slacks. "Almost done." She waved at the wheelbarrow, its blue paint obscured by filth. "Last load. Putting it on the garden. I'll till it under tomorrow."

He reached for the rope. Almost reluctantly, she let him have it. He twitched it to make the bucket tip and fill, hoisted, poured. When the barrow was full, he helped her fit the lid back onto the tank and fill in the hole. Then he took the barrow's handles and — carefully, for its load sloshed and surged — trundled it out back to Molly's garden. He worked in silence, except when she asked him, "Still at the university?" He laughed then. "Yes," he told her. "Still teaching literature to incorrigibles. Still. . . ."

"Still writing?" Her voice was softer.

"Still writing." And fame still eluded him, as it did her.

"I've got some cider inside, for when we're done."

They reached the garden. She stopped him when he began to tip the barrow. "I want to spread it," she explained, and she showed him. She dipped a bucket full of sludge and heaved it, a fanning spray of tarry gunk that would, come spring and summer, nourish her crops and herself. The breeze, still gentle, caught the stink. He gasped and stepped aside.

But he did not step far enough. The next bucketful caught him across the thighs.

She said, "Oh, sh — !"

He swore. He said, "Why don't you look where you're heaving that stuff?"

She made brushing motions with her hands, but she stopped herself before actually touching him. "Let's go inside. Get you cleaned up. I've got a washing machine, and there are still some of Nick's things." The words rushed from her mouth, driven by embarrassment.

"No, thanks." He spat the words, his voice bitter. He turned away, stalking, barely registering the water that came to her eyes, the hurt his rejection caused her. He would wash out his pants in the brook, and be damned to her!

She was just like his wife. His ex-wife. He had seen her through eight years of picking at childhood scabs. He had listened to her, soothed her, helped her all he could. He had suffered too, with her, for her, for himself. He had hoped it would all be worth it, that in time he would have joy in his marriage.

But when it was over, she had begun to make him miserable. She had done her best to treat him like a stranger. She had frozen him out. She had said that she no longer needed him. That she had grown beyond him.

She had taken their daughter, and she had left.

He had helped her clean out her septic tank, and she had rewarded him by dumping a bucket of shit over his head. And now Molly! Never again, never again would he expect reward for help. Not a mug of cider, not a smile, not . . . not love, from a woman.

It was not far to the brook, too short a distance and a time for his nose to grow used to the stench that rose from his pant legs, for his soul to grow calm. He found the path and left the road hurriedly, walked briskly past the field, through the thicket and the woods. He surveyed the pools and smiled. The trout were there indeed. They were, in fact, so many that it took him a while to find an empty pool in which to wash out his trousers.

While they soaked, he lit a fire beneath a low branch. When it was going well, he wrung out his pants and hung them to dry. Bare-legged then, he walked along the path, exploring the brook. There were plenty of trout. He could have all he wanted, all he could carry, and he would eat well this winter. He would come back that night.

He came to the clearing, still blighted, worse blighted. The wood stubble was gone. Now the ground was bare, nearly leafless even in autumn, worn as if by flood, cracked as if by drought or fire, dry and stony. The surrounding vegetation seemed to shrink away, its revulsion apparent in the lean of dry and broken stems. Oddly, a single tree grew in the middle of the clearing.

He circled that tree, examining it closely. It seemed healthy. There were buds on its twigs, and he could make out a few persistently clinging beech nuts. It seemed sturdy, and by its thickness it had been there many years. Why, he wondered, was it alone unaffected by whatever had blasted the soil around it? And why had he failed to notice it the last time he had passed this way?

He scanned the circle of the ground, and a circle it was. As near as he could tell, the tree sat in the precise center of the blighted zone. Was it a target? Or a source? And if so, if either, of what?

To one side he found a single intruding plant. A wild grape vine, withered by frost and, it seemed, by something else at its blackened tip, crossed from wood to clearing. Within the clearing, it bore a small cluster of gone-by grapes, the sour, purple kind called fox grapes.

He wondered, but his legs were cold. He shivered. He thought that by now his pants must be dry, or dry enough.

It lacked an hour of midnight when he returned. There was an old feed bag in his hand, and in it his net. When he unfolded it, he would hold an open-mouthed sack at the end of a three-foot handle. It was eminently suited for the task ahead, for it was still a week before the full moon, and there was not enough light for a spear.

His breath fogged in the darkness, and he was glad of his thick jacket. It was late, he was tired, and he felt the cold. His ears strained for footsteps in the brush, for voices in the distance, for the slam of a car door back at the road, for anything that suggested he might get caught. He was poaching, after all, out of season and with unsanctioned tools. He knew better, too. He was a college professor, wasn't he? But he had been raised not far from here, and his moral sense failed to jib at a little night-dipping. Too, his taste buds treasured fall-caught trout, legal or no.

The woods were not silent. There was the purling of water over the rocks, the rattling of branches in the breeze, a crackling that might have been a deer passing through a thicket, the small noises of the few small animals that were not abed or gone for the winter. There was a splash, and he started. He calmed himself deliberately, telling his pounding heart it was only a trout, leaping from one pool to another, or fending off a rival.

He unfolded the net, stepped softly onto a boulder beside a chute. He watched the swirling water, looking for the telltale bulge of a trout's back. He dipped the net into the pool, swept it with the current, felt it glance from solid flesh. He turned the sweep, and weight tugged at his hand. He raised the dripping net and grinned at his first fish. Six pounds, perhaps even seven. And there were plenty more.

He quit when he had a dozen in the sack. Not all were as big as his first, but he thought he had a generous forty pounds of trout for his freezer. He would enjoy them, every one, but he did wish he still had his family to share them with.

He had moved down the brook in his hunt, hopping from rock to rock, abandoning each pool when he frightened its occupants into hiding or flight. Now he hoisted the sack over his shoulder, net neatly folded and laid atop the fish, and stepped from stone to bank. He found the path and turned upstream again. He would have to be careful when he reached the road, he reminded himself. A warden might be prowling, headlights off. Fortunately, his clothes were dark and the woods were always near.

When he came to the clearing, he paused to shake and clear his head. He should have been in bed long since, but he did want the trout he carried. He glanced to the side. It was a mystery, how the ground stayed so bare when the air was full of falling leaves, how nothing grew there except the one lonely tree. He peered. Or was it so bare? He could make out blots of shadow scattered on the soil, leaves that must have fallen or blown since that afternoon.

He froze, suddenly watchful. He twitched his head from side to side, jumping his gaze from shadow to shadow. He backed down off the path into the inadequate concealment of an alder clump.

The woods had been quiet, but they had been alive with small noises. Now they were silent. No mice pattered through their runs beneath the leaves. No deer rattled twigs. It seemed that even the breeze had stilled and the brook had slowed its flow.

Why? There was something here that had not been here before. A warden? Maybe. Another poacher? Maybe. But why was there no sound of steps, of cloth brushing against leafless branches? He glanced at his watch. It was after midnight.

A shadow moved. Or did it only seem to move? He *was* tired, and he knew what waking dreams could be. He held his breath. It moved again, and a figure separated from it. It was tall and slender, clad in a soft, white gown of antique cut. It was beautiful and woman, and its beauty reminded him of his wife, of Molly, of all women at their bitterest. She was not at all an "it," though her face spoke volumes of disdain. She carried herself erect, her breasts thrust forward, her hips swayless, her belly flat. She was aloof, woman untouchable and isolate. She seemed a very goddess, though of what he could not guess.

He huddled among the alder stems as she stepped into the clearing. He watched as she gestured toward the ground-despoiling leaves, each gesture a languid wave, ending with an outthrust finger and a silent flare of light. Each leaf vanished in a puff of ash.

She paced her clearing, and he understood. She wanted no hint of green within her circuit, no reminder of life, even of life gone by. Or was that true? She paced near the grape vine and its shrunken offering. She gestured, but no finger pointed and no light flared. He thought he glimpsed the barest hint of a smile before she turned toward the tree.

He had thought he understood, but now he wondered. Mercy and humor had not lived in her face before she saw the vine, and they did not now. Cold and lovely, she faced the tree, arms and breasts lifted. She embraced the bark, and then, he thought, she merged with it, diffusing into the wood, donning the tree as she might a costume or a suit of armor.

She was a dryad, then. A dryad of the beech. A goddess, indeed. But she, or his dream, was gone now, and he did not linger. Once more shouldering his sack, he rose from the ground and stepped onto the path. He had to struggle not to run.

As he hurried away, he pondered what he thought he had seen. It was hard to believe, wholly beyond his modern context, but he had seen it. He had. Hadn't he? It was real, and it had been real for at least as long as the clearing had been dying. That meant two years, or more, and he thought of all the marriages that had turned sour in that time. Was she a plague for people as she was for leafy growth?

As he turned onto the deserted road, he guessed she was. Yet she had stayed her hand for a grape. Why? He doubted she loved anything but herself and her beechtree home. Had she appreciated the fruit as a seeming offering?

Was there a lesson in that for him? His ex-wife was beyond any renewal of courting. As the goddess did with leaves, she had turned the love they had shared to ashes. Any peace offering, any mute bid for mercy or a smile, she would reject. And, in truth, he no longer wanted her.

But Molly? He stopped in the road before her house. The windows were blank panes of glass, lightless and dark. A wisp of smnoke curled from the chimney, speaking of a fire smoldering against the night's chill. He liked her, he did. He thought she liked him. He smiled mirthlessly. And the bucket of sludge was behind them, not ahead.

He left the road. He stepped onto her drive, his feet crunching gravel. He walked to her porch and set down his sack. He thought a moment before pulling out his wallet and extracting an old receipt from the cleaners. He took a pen from his shirt pocket and wrote, "No hard feelings, Molly." He signed it, "Stinky," and then he laid it on the top step. He used a trout from his sack to weight down the note.

Refreshed, he whistled softly the rest of the way home. He had no thought for wardens, and tbey none for him.

The Bung-Hole Caper

The aliens came to Earth the same spring that Cyrus Holmes found the old barrel. It was buried under a stack of old lumber in a dark corner of the barn, and it would have stayed buried if Cyrus hadn't been looking for his grandfather's tool chest. Grandpa had been a cooper all his life, and when he was gone, the tools had been stored away. They included a cooper's adze, which Cyrus thought might be just the thing for roughing out a new plow handle.

He found the adze. Once sharpened, it worked as well as he had hoped. He also found the barrel, and that was in rather worse shape. It had been drying for half a century, forgotten in the shadows, and its staves now fitted as badly as fence pickets. But a month or two in the pond would fix that, he told Allie, his wife. Then he could replace the hoops and have a decent vessel to harden his cider in.

All through that summer, Cyrus tended the barrel. He soaked the wood in pond water, watching the wood swell and tighten. He replaced the hoops with cobblings from his workbench. He stood the thing in the yard, filled it from the hose, and watched as the last leaks slowed and stopped. Finally, it was as tight as it would ever be, and the apples in his small orchard weren't quite ready.

In the meantime, there were the aliens. Cyrus knew all about them. He didn't have a tractor or a chain saw or an electric milker. He worked his fields with a yoke of oxen, cut his firewood with an axe, and milked his dozen cows by hand. Still, he was up-to-date enough. He had a car, for getting to church of a Sunday and so Allie could drive to her job in town. He had a radio or two. He even had a teevee set, and he never missed the six-thirty news.

He knew all about the aliens. He'd seen pictures of them, all smothered in pastel-patterned coal-scuttle helmets, like something out of a movie about the Great War. He'd heard they were refugees from some foreign disaster or war, and he knew they were asking for a place to settle in the ocean shallows, promising not to interfere with navigation or fishing — they farmed their food on land — and offering to trade. They had science beyond anything Earth knew, they had technology, and they had a price list. The space for a small colony, a little place to call their own, for instance, was worth the plans for a space drive. Help in settling in was worth a map to worlds that men could live on. Other things were worth money, credits that could be exchanged for travel tickets, for lesser goods, even for alien encyclopedias, suitably translated. Earth was drooling.

Cyrus thought it all interesting enough, but he was a farmer, a raw-boned, weathered outcropping of Maine's coastal hills. The aliens scarcely touched his life, and they never would, any more than the rest of modern life did. Too, he'd never seen an alien. Not many people had, for though they traveled plenty, they did it in closed black limousines, chauffered by UN flunkies.

Cyrus — he hated being called "Cy" so much that anyone who dared be so familiar might get day-old eggs or half-soured milk — Cyrus put the aliens on a par with Florida hurricanes and California floods and Detroit strikes. They were all interesting. They all made the news. And he thought about them only when they crossed the flickering screen of his teevee set.

But the day came, it did. His apples ripened, and he gathered up the falls and picked the rest. He set a basket of the best down cellar for winter eating, helped Allie put up two dozen jars of applesauce, and filled the trailer with the bags and boxes that remained. Then he visited the cider mill.

The mill was Bob Witham's. An ancient rig of flapping belts and groaning gears, powered by a gasoline engine, it was nearly as decrepit as its toothless, flatulent owner. But it made good cider.

Cyrus binned his apples and watched the endless belt haul them up the chute to the grinder. As old Bob paddled the pulp into the burlapped flats for the press, Cyrus said, "Got a barrel now." He had to roar to be heard above the machinery.

Bob glanced up from his work. "Good for you."

"Ayuh. Old one. Found it out in the barn."

"Hope it's tight," Bob held up a hand to examine a gob of apple pulp sticking to a thumb. He licked it off. "Good apples this year, Cyrus."

"Should hope so. M'nured the bejeezus out of 'em. Soaked the barrel, too."

"Oughta do it. Stand back now." Bob threw a switch, and the grinder overhead groaned into silence. He flipped the last fold of burlap into place, laid a flat on top, and leaned into the pile of neatly wrapped squares of pulp. They rolled into the press on their dolly and jolted to a stop. He hauled on the lever that lowered the immense plate of the press into position. He flipped the lever that fed power to the belt that drove the press's screw. The screw turned. The plate mashed down. Juice spurted from the flats, collected in the gutters, and was pumped to the holding tank on the wall above their heads.

"Where's that cup?" asked Cyrus. Bob turned to point at the wall. There hung, just as it did every fall, a battered dipper. Once it had been enameled gray and blue. Now it was mostly rust, but Cyrus didn't mind. He took it off its nail and held it to catch the dripping cider. He drank deeply, and then he offered it to Bob. "It's good."

"Ayuh. Barrel'll do it more good'n them plastic jugs of yours, too."

"Hope so." The juice was sweet and tart, yet not too tart. Once hardened and settled, it would have a decent kick to it.

When the last drop of juice had left the press, Cyrus fetched his jugs from the car. They were the five-gallon inflatable things the hardware store sold to campers. Cyrus had found them good for cider, for maple sap at sugaring-off time, even for hauling water in dry spells. Now he puffed them open and held than under the hose from the holding tank. They filled slowly, since the hose was none too big, but he was in no great hurry. The cows would need milking when he got home, but they could wait for half an hour. Sixty gallons of cider was well worth a little patience.

He didn't unload the trailer till after supper. Between milking the cows in the pasture and the other chores, he had no time, and even then he didn't have enough. The barrel was in the barn, resting on its side, the bung-hole neatly plugged, its filling port on top and open. He ranged his jugs beside it. Then he selected one and took it into the house. "Fresh cider," he said to Allie. "Want a glass?" She did. They drank. They filled a pitcher for the fridge and put the rest in smaller jugs for the freezer. It would keep there,and they would have it for their grandchildren, for nieces and nephews, for themselves whenever they didn't care for hard cider. "I'll put the rest in the barrel tomorrow," he told his wife, "That's soon enough."

They refilled their glasses then, took them into their small living room, and turned on the news. And there were the aliens again, big as life. It seemed the French had sent them a case of wine. They liked it, asked for more, and paid, generously. "Our guests," said the teevee announcer, "have said they will pay for whatever they want. And we want their money, for only with it can we buy the wonders they have to sell. The trick has been finding things they want. We are very different creatures, with different tastes and different needs, and they are far ahead of us in technology. Too many of the things we make, they can make better, and they have less desire for our handicrafts than we have for Indian pots and blankets. After all, we aren't related." The announcer smiled, showing well-kept teeth.

Cyrus grunted. Allie said, "Maybe they would like your cider."

Cyrus grunted again. "Doubt it. 'Tain't wine, is it?" She agreed. Cider was a country thing that rarely appealed even to most humans, living as they did in cities. Most folks preferred wine and beer. Why should the super-civilized aliens be any different?

First thing next morning, as soon as the milking was done, Cyrus headed for the barn. He wanted to get his cider into his barrel, get it working with a touch of baker's yeast, get it started toward his favorite brew. But when he entered the barn, the barrel was not as he had left it. The bung hole was no longer plugged, and the barrel itself had rolled a bit.

He scratched his head. Had someone come last night to steal some cider? No. All the jugs were there, just as full as he had left them. He swore.

When the barrel twitched, he swore again. When he saw a movement behind the unplugged bung-hole, he did it once more. Damn! His cider barrel, that he was counting on to give him better drink, was occupied. A rat? A mouse? It was late in the year for snakes, and birds would never enter such a place.

There was a sound, like a watery voice. The movement repeated, and a ropy thing, a tentacle, emerged from the bung-hole. With difficulty, he realized what he had. An alien. Of all things. What was it doing here? Where was its chauffeur? Where was its shell? He traded his puzzlement for a growing anger. What right did it have to take over his barrel, to deny him proper cider?

The tentacle wriggled. "Please, excuse," the voice burbled, echoing within the barrel. "Shell, too-small. Abandoned, vehicle. Seek, other."

Cyrus hunkered down. He peered into the bung-hole, trying to make out a detail or two. It was too dark in there, but he glimpsed what might have been an eye, a damp hide, a lobsterish mouth. By all accounts, the things were harmless enough. He didn't fear, and his anger was fading, already giving way to fascination.

The tentacle writhed. It tapped the end of the barrel above the bung-hole. It tapped twice, once to either side. "Make," the voice burbled again. "Holes. Eyes." It tapped below, along the barrel's curving flank. "Legs."

There was a pause while Cyrus thought it over. The creature didn't speak the language well, but it could get its wishes across well enough. Cyrus knew what it wanted, all right. But he knew, too, that boring all those holes would ruin the barrel. He'd be stuck with plastic cider for another year, and maybe longer. Finally, the voice spoke again. "Will, pay," it said.

That was another matter. "All right," said Cyrus. "Though I want to know why you chose my barrel." He stood and headed for his workbench. He found his electric drill and the hole saw. He added over his shoulder, "How big you want the holes?"

When the voice said, "This," he turned to watch the tentacle sketch a two-inch circle. Fine, he thought. The saw could handle that. He plugged in the extension cord and fetched his equipment back to the barrel. "Back off, now," he said. The tentacle withdrew, and he pulled the trigger. The saw bit and whined, once, twice, and the alien had eye holes. As he sat back on his heels, the eyes appeared. They were on stalks, and they were extended a good six inches out the holes. "Thank," the alien said. "See, now." The voice still burbled, but it echoed less. The new holes made a difference

"Now," said Cyrus. The barrel wasn't really ruined yet. He could always fit a new top to it. But now. . . . "Where do you want those leg holes?"

Once more the tentacle emerged. It lengthened, more than he would have guessed possible, and it pointed. The saw whined again, six times, and the job was done. Or was it? Cyrus thought a moment and said, "You want more room around that arm of yours?" When the tentacle quickly sketched an oblong around the bung-hole, he obliged.

He rose, put his tools away, and returned. The head of his barrel now reminded him of nothing more than a Halloween pumpkin, all eyes and mouth, though no pumpkin ever had stalked eyes and a mouthful of wormy tentacles. No pumpkin had legs either, shiny and lobsterish, emerging from holes in its bottom. And no pumpkins walked, with a lurching, rocking gait, sideways across the barn floor. It struck him then, that the aliens resembled hermit crabs, wearing borrowed shells and moving into larger ones as they grew. He wondered if a real hermit crab might try a pumpkin.

He watched as the alien exercised its limbs. It crawled, it ran, it even capered as it grew used to its new shell, but it remained clumsy. A barrel just wasn't built to walk. Finally, it settled again, facing Cyrus, and burbled, "Thank."

Cyrus almost grinned. He prided himself on rarely going into a flap, no matter what the crisis. And he had a crisis here, for sure. An alien, away from its people, free of its human guides and chauffeurs. It would have to go back, of course. It would probably want to, unless it preferred a holiday among the natives. In the meantime, well. . . . "Mind if I call you Hermit?"

There was no answer. He added, "It's time to talk, you know. Why my barrel?"

The tentacles withdrew. In a moment they returned to scatter a handful of plastic strips on the floor before the man. The alien money. One tentacle retained a strip and held it up. "Pay. New, shell. Food?"

"Soon," said Cyrus. "But first, why?" Damn, he thought. It's got me doing it too. Though it's not hard. We do talk that way here, a bit.

"Found, first." The alien's burble was somehow plaintive. "Hungry." Cyrus said nothing. After a moment, the alien went on. "Grow, we. Shells, change, always. Small, natural. Bigger, smarter, plastic. Change, must. Too-weak, not. Too-soft."

Cyrus stared intently, thinking beginning to see. . . . He was interrupted by a gasp. He turned, and there was Allie, a hand to her mouth, an apron around her waist. "I wanted the eggs," she said. "What's that?"

He told her. She scooched beside him, staring too. "They grow all their lives," he said. "Move into bigger shells as they grow. It says they get smarter too. I guess the brain must get bigger as they grow."

She nodded. Her gray hair bobbed. Her thin lips pursed. She smelled of the kitchen and soap. Her thigh was soft against his haunch, and he remembered. . . . The past, their past, was far from dead, but though he still loved her, she wasn't the girl he had married, the girl who had left him for college and then returned for a farmer's life. She said, murmuring, "I suppose it must have been learning how to build their own shells that let them get smart enough for civilization, then."

"Skin," the alien burbled. "Wood. Metal. Plastic. Food?"

"What would you like?" asked Allie.

"Egg? Cheese? Potato, mash?"

"Right away." She rose to her feet, as graceful as ever, and headed toward the back of the barn and the door to the hen house. In a minute she was back, an egg in her hand. She laid it down before the barrel. A tentacle enfolded it and hauled it within. There was a crunch and a sound of sucking. "Thank."

"They aren't very big today, are they?" said Allie. She left again. While she was gone, Cyrus peered through the widened bung-hole. Despite the holes, it was still dark in there, and he had to lean close to make out the broken egg, cradled in a nest of tentacles beneath a writhing mass of mouthparts. He leaned too close, in fact, for when the alien was done, the discarded shell bounced off his brow. He rocked back on his haunches with a muttered curse. "No manners," he said. "None at all."

"Whatever do you mean?" asked Allie. She was back, standing behind him, her apron sagging with the weight of eight more eggs. "Maybe you shouldn't have been prying. I imagine it likes its privacy as much as we do."

"Then it should have stood at home."

"Enough of that, Cyrus!" She scooched beside the barrel and laid her eggs down on the floor. She held one out toward the bung-hole. "Would you like another?"

"Thank." A tentacle plucked the egg from her grasp. There was another crunching, sucking sound. She added, "It's a stranger, Cyrus. Away from home, and it probably doesn't know how it's going to get back. We should be nice to it."

"I suppose we should, Allie." They had always been as hospitable as they knew how, with friends and strangers alike. Every winter saw at least one stranded motorist warming himself before their stove and dining at their table, even passing the night in their guest-room bed. But never before had they hosted a stranger as strange as this one. "But I am curious."

"I know. I don't think anyone's seen them naked."

The alien had obviously been listening. "No," it burbled, discarding the second eggshell. "Fear. Eat, be. Call? Phone?"

"You want us to call your friends? At the UN?"

"Yes. Please. Thank."

As they stood, another egg disappeared into the bung-hole. "I'll just leave them all," said Allie. "The poor thing's probably hungry."

"Enough, now. Take."

"All right." Allie gathered up the remaining eggs, and they turned to leave, thinking the alien would stay put. But as Cyrus was holding the door to the kitchen for his wife, they heard a scrabbling behind them. They looked, and there was the barrel, lurching along on six shiny legs, stalked eyes waving as they took in the yard, the car, the oxen behind their rail fence.

"We haven't had a dog for years," said Cyrus. "Wish we could keep it."

"Cyrus!"

The word got out, of course. By the time the limousine arrived, the yard was choked with neighbors, townsfolk, and local reporters. There was even a wire-service helicopter in the pasture. Their alien was the center of attention, and it was loving it. It burbled happily away, posing for pictures, answering questions, and making comments. At one point, its gist seemed to be that its new shell reminded it acutely of a precious antique it had had to leave at home. "Hurry," it burbled sadly. "Danger. Fear. Leave, all. Now, new. Bigger!"

When the car pulled in, honking aside the crowd, the alien turned to watch, raising itself to the tips of its legs. It was silent as the driver, a young black man uniformed in powder blue, jumped out, saying, "What's been happening?" It remained silent as three of its fellows emerged from the back seat. They wore the coal-scuttle shells everyone knew from the teevee, and they were small, no larger than a bushel basket. When they saw the barrel, they sank on their legs, just as if they were bowing. They didn't speak, though it seemed natural to think they would have come armed with more than one choice phrase for their runaway.

The barrel lurched toward its smaller fellows. They flinched, retreating toward the car. "Up!" it burbled. "Home. Now!"

The others scurried. "Master!" they chorused. Their voices piped liquidly, and Cyrus thought their shells must have very different acoustics from his barrel. Their attitude puzzled him, too, until Allie jogged his elbow with her own and said, "It's so much bigger. That must be it."

"They think it's smarter!"

She nodded. She turned toward one of the reporters and told him what they had learned. "If size and intelligence go together, then the bigger ones must be the leaders."

The reporter, a fiftyish man with a bulbous nose and white hair, answered in a whiskey voice. "Then you must have the boss-bug of them all here. I've never seen a bigger one."

Cyrus said; "It's just the barrel." He noticed the patch on the reporter's sleeve. The symbol was the same as the one on the helicopter. "Though I suppose it gives it plenty of room to grow."

They turned their attention back to the aliens as the newcomers scrambled nimbly into the limousine. The barrel followed, just managing to squeeze through the door. It was a tight fit, and Cyrus was glad his barrel hadn't been any bigger. Or was he? He was sorry to see the alien go. He'd been counting on that barrel for his cider, and, besides, he rather liked the alien. It was such a peculiar little bugger.

The fuss died down soon enough. There was better local news, such as the flying saucers seen near the nuclear power plant in Wiscasset, and the aliens were drawing more attention with their request for a piece of the Florida Keys for their colony. The ocean was shallow enough there, they said; the islands would give them enough land for their needs, and the climate was much like that they had left. The locals, of course, wouldn't hear of it, but the rest of the world didn't think the spot a bad idea at all. At least, so said the teevee.

But the story didn't end there. The limousine was back before Thanksgiving, bearing a silk-suited diplomat and an alien whose wooden barrel was now smoothed and polished and covered with the pastel patterns that denoted rank or, perhaps, identity among its kind. It looked more like a dressed-up pumpkin than ever.

The diplomat introduced himself as Vince Barger, the Second Assistant Under-Secretary for Alien Relations. "A new department, you understand," he added with a smile that kept his teeth carefully covered. "We try to mediate between K-ssniskit's people and our own."

"Snickit?" asked Cyrus.

"K-ssniskit. Didn't she tell you her name before?"

Cyrus shook his head, wrinkling his nose at a strong whiff of Barger's cologne. "Can't say she did. Though she didn't seem to like what I called her much. Thought she was sorta like a hermit crab."

"So he called her Hermit," put in Allie.

All three watched the alien as she moved around the yard, stalked eyes peering into barn, pasture, and house, renewing her brief acquaintance with the place. She must have grown used to the weight of the barrel, for she no longer lurched. She must also, thought Cyrus, have grown a little.

Barger chuckled smoothly. "I can see why. But you probably irritated her. They're very sociable creatures, really.'

He stopped talking when the alien scuttled closer. She stopped at Cyrus's feet and cocked her eyes up at his lanky figure. "Greet," she burbled.

"Greet, yourself." Cyrus squatted to be nearer her level. "What're you after now?"

"Cyrus!" said Allie. She turned to the alien. "Don't you mind him, K-ssnickit," she said. "We are glad to see you, and if we can do anything to help, we will." She bent to lay a hand on the rim of the barrel just above the eyes. She looked as if she were petting it.

"Greet," the alien repeated. "Shells, like." A tentacle stretched to stroke the barrel's flank. "More. Make?"

"I suppose I could," said Cyrus. "Grandpa's coopering tools are still in the barn, and he taught me a little when I was a boy."

"Thin. Light. Polish, too. Sizes, many. Two, thousand," K-ssniskit burbled.

Cyrus whistled. That was a lot of barrels. "Take time," he said. "What'll you pay?"

Barger held out a piece of paper. "Here's the order," he said. "Fifteen hundred dollars apiece, as long as you meet the specifications. We pay you, and they'll pay us."

Cyrus whistled again. He took the paper, unfolded it against its crisp resistance, and read. "Ayuh." He turned to look at Allie. She showed nothing but approval in her face. And they could surely use the money. "I suppose I might," he said. "But why me?"

"She insisted."

And that was that. Or almost that. Cyrus took the order, though at first he felt a little as he guessed a Navajo must feel, selling pots and blankets to jet-borne tourists. But he soon realized that it wasn't *his* heritage he was selling. He was more like a Hong Kong Chinaman making colonial trivets for Williamsburg shops.

Not that he minded, except for one thing. He was fast growing rich, he was honing long-forgotten skills, he was indulging a love for different woods and finishes, but he never seemed to have the time to make a barrel for himself. He still had to harden his cider in those damned plastic jugs.

Movers and Shakers

I'm no great shakes. Not for looks. Not for smarts. I've never claimed otherwise. How could I? I make my nut with a battered pickup, moving furniture, junk, garbage, whatever folks'll hire me for. Maybe you've seen my ad: "Light Hauling. Cheap. Reliable. Call 382-5877." It's nothing much, but it feeds me and pays the rent. I'm not married, never have been. Never could find a girl who wanted much to do with me, but then that's one expense I haven't got.

But the alien didn't know all that. I thought. There he was, three feet high, sitting or standing or squatting, whatever he called it, on my doorstep. One squirmy looking finger, like an octopus' arm except it didn't have any suckers, was still hanging in the air where the knocker had been until I opened the door. His eyes, black and wet, with no whites, were buried in folds of scaly skin. He looked like a cross between a fish and a squid. Smelled like one too. He sounded like — like God knows what. Think of an accordion that's been soaked for a month in molasses. That's not quite it, but it'll give you the flavor of it. His voice was slow and sticky, and it came out of a hole about where you'd expect a mouth to be.

The alien was saying something, but I wasn't hearing. I was staring. I'd read enough sci-fi to know this thing in front of me was an alien. It had to be, though blobs like this had been out of style since the thirties. And even then people had preferred aliens that looked at least vaguely human. Maybe I'd been drinking too much lately?

Too much booze in me or not, this thing was no hallucination. When I didn't answer him right away, he reached out and touched me on the chest with a finger. Or was it an arm? As far as I could see, it and fifty others just like it emerged directly from the creature's side.

That made them arms, right?

He touched me again, in the general neighborhood of the empty buttonhole over my navel. I stopped gaping and said, "What do you want?" Very intelligent of me, but then I told you I wasn't much on smart. Besides, I wasn't altogether cool, calm, and collected at the moment.

"You are over your shock, yes? You have never seen my like before, but you can accept me, yes?" His wheeze was hard to listen to, but I could make it out. He was right, too. I could accept him, at least until he tried to crawl back into a bottle. I nodded vaguely and stepped aside. I waved him inside the door, gaping again when I saw how he moved. Like a centipede on all those arms. Or were they fingers? It really was better that he get inside out of sight. There was no telling what the neighbors would say if they saw him. Get me jugged, for sure. Keeping wild animals, dangerous pets, public nuisances, or something — if they didn't riot. It was a crummy neighborhood, but good enough so everyone could look down on me.

I closed the door behind him and followed him into the living room. Bedroom, too, for that matter, and kitchen. I sat down on the edge of the couch I used for a bed and waited for him to say something else.

"Call me Wirtz," he said.

"I'm Fordy." Then, thinking he might want something more formal, I added, "Sanford Randall. Tbough folks just call me Fordy."

"I know this. I also know you are illegitimate and have an IQ of 93. You are a virgin, an alcoholic, and a peeping tom. You shoplift, cheat on your taxes, and chisel more welfare than you deserve. You are also thirty-eight years old. I checked you out."

Speaking of peeping! And all I knew was that he was an ugly, nosy snob. I didn't like him much. "So what do you want?"

"I am a scholar. An experimental scholar. It is my calling to study primitive planets such as this one, to determine the quantal bits in their folklore and to cause the natives to act them out. I then record the results and publish them as holo films on my home world of Calaz. They are quite popular."

I didn't understand more than one word in three, but I got the idea. He was a meddler, like the anthrowhatevers who poke around the jungle gooks right here on Earth. He made money out of it too. Well, as long as a little of it rubbed off on me, he could study me all he wanted. "So where do I come in?" I said.

"These quantal bits — I have determined them already for your culture." A ripple ran through the boneless arms on one side of his body — his equivalent of a shrug? — and a slit opened in his skin. He reached in and pulled out what looked like a small sheet of paper. He held it up in front of his eyes and read aloud from it: "Penny pincher. Food for thought. Rubble rouser. Father knows best. Movers and shakers." He tucked the paper away again and went on. "That will do for a sample, yes. The last is you."

"Movers and shakers? You're going to make a mover and shaker out of me?" Fat chance! Like I said at the beginning, I'm no great shakes, and I know it. He'd have a better chance of making a silk purse out of a pig's ear.

"Not make one, no. You already are one. A mover because that is how you make your living, yes? And a Shaker because of your grandmother."

Oh, grandma. She turned Shaker about three years after she qualified as my grandma. Grandpa spent the next five years splitting his time between raising my mom, earning a living, and trying to convince her to come home. Then he divorced her and married again. All I could say was, "She makes me a Shaker too?"

"As much as anyone I could find who was a mover too. But now I must gain your cooperation. It is my understanding that movers and shakers become political leaders, found large corporations, or make great fortunes, and I cannot make you do any of those things. I need your help." That shrug again, but this time no pockets opened. Maybe he just didn't like admitting he couldn't do everything himself. Not that my help would be worth much. I'd never been able to make a fortune for myself, not that I hadn't wished hard enough.

I told him as much, adding that this called for a drink. I leaned over and fetched a bottle out from under the couch. Good booze. The last of a case I'd found squirreled away in a basement I was cleaning out two weeks ago. "Want any?"

"Ethanol agrees with me. We will drink to our partnership, yes?" I nodded at him and found a couple of glasses on the windowsill. I poured, and we both knocked the stuff back. He didn't have any more trouble with it than I did. He wasn't all that alien. He even liked it. His first words on getting the slug down were, "More, yes?"

I poured again, and we got down to business. He stretched out on tbe floor, on his back, those fifty-odd arms wiggling in the air except for the two that braced the glass on his chest. His head was between my feet, so that his eyes looked up at me whenever I looked down. I kept my eyes on my own glass as much as I could.

As soon as he was comfortable, he said, "Some ideas from you, yes? What do you wish to movc and shake?"

I didn't have any use for politics, and — really — I was okay without gobs of money. It would just go for more booze, until I drowned in the stuff. But here he was, lookiny like a whole can of angle worms escaped from a fish factory. If I could just get him to run across the sidewalk when. . . . "Well, there's this broad lives down the street. . . ."

"The one you were watching three nights ago, yes?"

Yeahh! "That's right."

"No." He waved his glass at me. "More, please, yes." I poured. I gave myself a splash more while I was at it. "That is not what I mean. A mover and sbaker affects the world, not individuals, yes? You need to have bigger plans."

Bigger plans. And I was pretty happy the way I was. But that wouldn't do. This alien, this Wirtz, he called himself, wanted to make something of me. I hadn't run into that since my mom died. "But I don't want that much," I said. "I've got about all I need right now."

He sighed, I swear it. Then he shrugged and opened another pocket. He reached in and pulled out a little sac. He opened the sac and spilled it out onto the floor beside him. I stared, even more than when I'd first seen him. Gold nuggets. Diamonds. Rubies. Jewels I'd never heard the names for. Small ones, though. Nothing big. Nothing flashy.

"First you will sell these. I have more if you need them, in my ship. Tben you will buy some good clothes. Suits and shirts and shiny shoes, yes? More of this excellent ethanol, too. Then you will expand your business."

I must have looked blank, for he sighed again. "You coUect garbage, yes? So you will buy a real garbage truck." And he laid it out. He had it all figured. He would make me the garbage king of the county, even the state. First the clothes, to make me look like a prosperous business man. Then the truck, business loans, more trucks, drivers, until I was a goddam monopolist. And then I'd bid to handle the city landfill, cheap, bring in sorting equipment, and start selling scrap metal, glass, and so on. The perfect garbage operation. No dump problem, total recycling, and we could even process the garbage that had already been buried. All I needed was him to steer me along and his diamonds to finance it all.

By now the bottle was almost empty and my head was whirling, more from Wirtz than the booze. I'd had less than half the bottle. Considerably less. He'd had the rest. So I agreed. I'd go along. I'd stooge for him, and I wouldn't have any illusions about it all. He'd really wanted my ideas? Don't make me laugh!

It went just the way he'd laid it out. I sold a small diamond to a fence I knew, no questions, bought the clothes, and took the rest of the sparklers to a legit jeweler in another town. Got a good price that way. Bought the truck then, hired a man, and spent my time bidding cheap on restaurant contracts. Got enough of them so I needed more trucks and talked the bank into buying them. Had the city monopoly in a year, took over the landfill, and that was when Wirtz crawled out from under my couch, where he'd been boozing it up all along. He'd only come out for a fresh bottle or to hand me some more of his jewels.

Now, though, he wanted to take a real hand in the operation. He had me get a big pet carrier, one of those plastic-covered masonite boxes with a window in one end, and take him out to the landfill. Once we were there, he had me carry him around and show him the joint. That was a chore! The place was an old gravel pit, a hole in the ground most of a quarter mile across, half of it filled in with everybody's leavings. I bitched at having to lug him around, but he just said, "Do you want people to see me, no?" No way! I had the money now, but I still hadn't moved. Too much trouble. So the neighbors could still riot.

He didn't explain himself until we'd covered the ground twice. Then he told me, "You will set up the sorting machines over there, where there is no garbage yet. Then you will only need a conveyer to get what has already been buried."

And that's the way it was. I had to have a road bulldozed for the trucks, so they could get around to the back of the landfill pile, and I had to have foundations built for the machinery. But within six months I was all set up; godawful great hoppers that fed the garbage to a shredder, magnets that yanked out the iron and steel, air blowers that separated out the paper and other light crap, shaking screens that sifted out the crushed glass, and a baler for the bits of copper wire, aluminum tubing, and the like tha came out at the end. I took one look at the finished noise-maker and named my outfit "Movers and Shakers, Inc." Wirtz had done it, alright. That's what I was. And I had more money than I'd ever dreamed existed. I got paid for picking up the garbage and then I turned around and sold it again. The paper went to a paper company. The glass went to a bottle maker. The metal went to a scrap metal dealer. A healthy profit on every ton, and more going out than my trucks were hauling in, at least until I'd finished sorting out the fifteen years worth of garbage that was buried behind the shredder.

That was when Wirtz came from under the couch again. He said he was bored. He wanted something to do, yes. And it was time to start recording how I was acting out the folklore quantum he had assigned me. He wanted a control room, set up right over the conveyer that brought the stuff out of the landfill. He wanted to be able to start or stop the whole show, or any part of it. He also wanted a grab-arm, like on a pulp truck, so he could pick things out of the garbage stream. As he put it, "There is no sense in letting a rock into the crusher, yes?"

How could I argue? That machinery was expensive. He got his control room, an air-conditioned metal box, four by four by four, with one window looking straight down on tbe conveyer. How he expected to movies that way, I didn't know, but that was what he wanted and it was none of my business anyway. Maybe he had a camera that could see through walls. That would explain how he'd known so much about me.

As long as I knew him after that, he stayed in that box. I brought him booze and food, whatever he asked for, and let him shut the conveyor down when he wanted to sleep. I hung around in the evenings, too, just to talk the way we had when he was living under my couch. I told him how things were going, how other towns were beginning to copy our setup, how the power company was talking about building a small plant near us to burn the paper and other combustibles we sorted out. If they did, we'd get a better price. Coal was more valuable than wood pulp, and that's what we'd be competing with. I bitched about all the paperwork too. I said I wanted to hire a lawyer to handle it for us. He said no. I should do it myself. It was good for me, yes? He sounded just like my mom.

I must have messed up the paperwork, though, because it wasn't long before we had an OSHA inspector checking us out. He looked at everything, talked to the employees, and filled out wads of forms. When he was done, he ticked me off for not haviny seat belts in the trucks, not having a railing around the shredder, not this, and not that. He said if I didn't make the place safer, I'd be paying fines, so much a day until I was "in compliance."

And then he asked me what that box over the conveyer was. So what could I do? I told him. "It's a control room."

"Not that small, it isn't. Unless you're violating the child labor laws too." He was a smartass, he was. But then weren't they all?

"No kids," I protested. And then I put my foot in it. "No midgets or dwarfs, either."

"So who runs it? I don't see you paying anyone enough to squeeze himself in there." He paused for a moment. Then he hauled his sheaf of forms out of his pocket again and said, "Maybe you'd better let me have a look inside."

I backed off, quick. "Why bother? It's just machinery inside, you know? Automated." Oh boy! I didn't want him seeing Wirtz. Not at all. He was trouble enough already, and I sure didn't want the feds walking off with my diamond supply. They would, too, if they realized what it was.

But he insisted. "I see a door. Open it up."

So I did. I didn't say another word while we walked the few yards across to Wirtz's little metal box. I led him right up to the door and opened it. And when he turned white I was too busy laughing to pay much attention to Wirtz's look of surprise. "What is it?" he gasped.

"It's a sea cucumber." I crossed my fingers.

"The hell it is." He straightened up, the color coming back to his face. I closed the door again. Wirtz would have to wait for an explanation. "The hell it is."

"Sure it is. I caught him off Cape Cod. Trained him to spot rocks and keep them out of the shredder."

"The hell you did. That's no sea . . . that's . . . not that big. Not with all those legs."

"So you tell me. Maybe I don't know a sea cucumber from a sea cabbage. Anyway, it's a trained animal." If he would swallow that, I was okay. The worst he could do was sic the SPCA on me.

"Yeah. A trained animal." He shook his head. I could see he didn't know what to think. Fumes from all the garbage, maybe? He'd probably wind up passing the buck to his boss, but it would be a few days before he got back to the office. We had a little time anyway.

As I walked him back out to the parking lot, I heard the conveyer speed up. Wirtz had probably heard it all, the damn peeper, but why should he be in a hurry now? Speeding up his cameras wouldn't get him done and out of the way any faster. Besides, the conveyer wasn't a camera.

Once I was rid of the snoop, I headed back to Wirtz as fast as I could, but it didn't do me any good. He was hunched over his window, staring down at the garbage zipping by on the conveyer twice as fast as usual. He was concentrating so hard I don't think he even heard me shouting at him. So I just watched, while he touched controls to speed up the shredder to keep up with the conveyer and the sorters to keep up with the shredder. By then I couldn't hear myself think, much less shout, so I headed back to the office: soundproofed, thank God.

Wirtz was more of a puzzle than I'd ever stopped to think. It had taken the OSHA guy to show me that. If I wasn't a boozer from way back, I might haved reacted like him the day Wirtz showed up on my doorstep. But I didn't. And now look at me. A businessman. An industrialist, yet. Getting rich, even. It was like having a fairy godmother. But how leng was it going to last? Wirtz was in a hurry now, which meant he intended or hoped to be done soon, probably before the snoops came back. I had to wonder if I could hack it without him. I certainly never had before.

As it turned out, it was a good two weeks before the feds came back, and by then the control room was a comfortable ten by twelve by eight, occupied by a college kid picking up a little cash for the fall. Wirtz, you see, had been done in ten days.

Four or five days before the feds showed up again, I came to work and found the place quiet. Shut down. Nothing running. Piles of garbage beside the hoppers where the trucks had dumped their loads. And the door to the control room wide open.

I walked — walked, hell, I ran — over to ask Wirtz what he was up to. Was he molting or mmething? But I never got a chance to open my mouth. The control room was empty. Wirtz was gone. In his place, Iying on the control room floor beside the window, was a piece of paper.

It was an apology. Wirtz, it seemed, was no scholar. He was a shipwreck. He'd been cruising over town one night when a piece of his engine fell off. It wasn't much, just a little doohickey that looked like a piece of twisted pipe and let him go home in a month instead of a century, so he had been able to land safely and hide his ship. But when he went looking for the doohickey, he couldn't find it. It was moving through the city, his instruments told him, faster than he could move without his ship. He caught up with it when it stopped moving, though, and found it buried under ten feet of garbage and fill, well beyond his solitary reach. So he had found me and set things up so he could search the whole damned landfill if he had to. And he had finally found his doohickey. Now he was on his way home, but he'd be back. And I should have a bottle waiting.

I laughed. I'd been had, conned by a friendly little boozer just my style. I looked forward to seeing him again. In the meantime, I was off my uppers for a change. I'd gotten as much out of it as he had. And I could get a little more, too, if I could just get on the stick and get that control room replaced in time.

It took two days and a lot of overtime to get the new structure built. Two-by-fours and plywood and tarpaper. The same air conditioner. The same controls, though with bigger handles. Windows in the walls in addition to the one in the floor. And it was worth it. When the OSHA guy came back, he was totally confused. Had he been seeing things? I could see the answer in his buddies' faces: he must have, with the story he'd been telling, and he wouldn't have his job all that much longer.

I'd been had, sure, but so had he. I'd passed it on, and that's what makes life bearable.

About the Author

Thomas A. Easton is a member of the Science Fiction and Fantasy Writers of America and a well-known science fiction critic (he has had a monthly book review column in the SF magazine *Analog* for over twenty years). Novels currently available from Wildside Press include *Sparrowhawk, Greenhouse, Woodsman, Tower of the Gods, Seeds of Destiny, Alien Resonance, Unto the Last Generation,* and *Stones of Memory. Silicon Karma* appeared from White Wolf in 1997.

He holds a doctorate in theoretical biology from the University of Chicago and is Professor of Life Sciences at Thomas College in Waterville, Maine. His work on scientific and futuristic issues has appeared in numerous magazines and journals. His most recent nonfiction book is *Taking Sides: Clashing Views on Controversial Issues in Science, Technology, and Society* (Guilford, CT: Dushkin, 4th ed., 2000).

Printed in the United States
65076LVS00003B/138

9 781587 152559